BILLIONAIRE
BY THE BOOK

NIKKI STEELE

ABOUT THIS BOOK

This book is an **Erotic Romance**. It contains strong, explicit, smoking hot sex scenes. It was previously published under the title *Books & Billionaires*.

CONTENTS

1. By the Book   9

2. By the Letter   55

3. By the Sea   101

4. By the Way   161

    Epilogue   203

    Author's Note   205

    Further Reading   206

DEDICATION

To KS. The love of my life, the inspiration for my dreams, the editor of my madness, the fire under my feet. Thank you for being, well… you

PART 1:

BY THE BOOK

A Librarian in a small town, Clara's heart broke three years ago. Now she lives in a world of books and rules to ensure it never happens again.

The only part of her still free is her imagination, living out the fantasies in her head that she can never have in real life.

But her safe life changes when a mysterious stranger takes shelter from a storm in her library. Stuck together for the night, will he be able to break down her walls? And if he does, what will be the consequences?

CHAPTER ONE

*"**My library book** is overdue," growled the tall, ripped man before me. His biceps flexed, straining against his tailored shirt as he clasped his collar, ripping it open. Rippled, perfect chest and abs were revealed underneath. "Perhaps we can think of some other way for me to pay my fines."*

On some level, I knew this was a daydream. I'd always had them; little scenarios that played out in my mind whenever I was alone, little voice overs to the conversation I was really having when in company. I wasn't crazy; it was just, when you looked more like *War and Peace* than *Reader's Digest*, opportunities for fun were limited. Sometimes you had to make your own.

Lately the daydreams had been growing… sexier. A byproduct perhaps of the fact that my birthday was fast approaching and, once again, I had no-one but my collection of paperbacks to share it with.

I visualized my man with slightly bigger biceps. Ooh yes, that was it. Now where was I? *His book was overdue.*

"But it's the rules," I breathed. "How else will you pay the fine?"

I imagined his hands going down to his belt. I could see it in my head; knew what was waiting underneath.

"Go on," he said." You know you want to. Right here in the library."

Was it getting hot in here? "What do you have in mind?"

He gently pulled the books I had been holding from suddenly lifeless fingers. "Let me help you stack the shelves."

"Make sure they're in order," I growled. "Or I might be forced to spank you."

"Hello? Anyone here?" My daydream was interrupted by a call from the front of the library.

Seriously? This was the good part. He never *got the hang of the Dewey Decimal system.*

I sighed, then got to my feet from where I'd been stacking books among the shelves. "We're closing." Not a single soul all day—not even a phone call—and then this.

"Hello?" the voice was persistent.

"We're closing!" I called, louder. I started to walk toward the front counter. "You'll have to come back-"

I stopped. "Oh." My throat was suddenly dry. I had to clear it before I could speak. "How can I help you?"

The stranger was slightly taller than me, well-built in an expensive suit; face clean shaven, but hair tousled. Gorgeous in that tall, dark and very handsome 'just walked off a photoshoot' sort of way. I did a brief double take, closing my eyes and then opening them to make sure I wasn't still dreaming.

Nope, this was real. Snow was melting off his shoulders and starting to pool on my freshly vacuumed floor. Wet carpet was *not* a fantasy I had ever entertained.

He seemed overly pleased to see me. "I'm wondering if I can borrow your landline – my cell isn't working, what with the storm outside."

"You don't want to borrow a book?"

He looked at me, confused. "No, thank you. I think there are more important things to be concerned about right now."

"Oh." I hadn't been outside all day. Must be one heck of a storm. I walked to the phone and picked it up, holding it out. "No long distance calls please, and I'll ask that you be quick, we're closing and my boyfriend will be here any minute now. He's a footballer, just so you know."

He raised an eyebrow, but took the phone with a gracious nod. "Thank you."

I walked down to collect my cart while the stranger made his call. To my thoughts, the library was a little like Mary Poppins' handbag: larger on the inside than it looked, and you just never knew what you might find once you dipped your hand within.

We'd been shoehorned into an old, grey, concrete building on the grounds of the local park, and shared our space with a community café at the front; the library accessible via a long corridor down one side lined with generic 'reading is fun' posters.

I loved it—it was my own little world of castles and kings, mysteries and mayhem. I could lose myself in these walls; escape my one room apartment with its TV dinners, and get paid to do it.

When I heard the stranger leave I made my way forward to lock the front door.

Didn't even say goodbye. That was handsome guys for you—nothing like the Prince Charming of my childhood novels… or my dreams.

"Until tomorrow, my love."

"Oh please, you don't really mean that."

"I do. Now that I know you're here, I'll be back every day. We won't make eye contact—we don't want the others to get suspicious—but I'll scribble notes to you in the margins of your favorite book."

I switched out the lights as I imagined the conversation playing out in my mind.

"Then one day you'll pick the book up and I'll be there, and our eyes will meet and-"

The front door burst open and I screamed, jarred out of my daydream by a figure clothed in black and white, snow swirling around his feet like a ghostly aura.

Books and handbag launched from my hands.

"Son of a biscuit, you startled me!"

Belatedly I recognized the outline before me. The stranger from before was back.

He chuckled. "My apologies. I didn't mean to scare you."

The warm laugh set me instantly at ease. "Is everything okay? Can I help you?"

"Yes actually, you can," the stranger replied. "I'm hoping you'll let me go home with you."

Was I daydreaming again? It was always like that: my mind saying the things I was too afraid to say out loud, doing the things the rules I had built around myself wouldn't let me do.

But this had been out loud. I couldn't be daydreaming!

"I'm sorry?" I said. "Could you repeat that please?"

He only then realized what he had said. "Oh. Oh my God, no. I'm so sorry—not like that. I meant, can I get a lift home with you? And your boyfriend?"

A little spark died. "Boyfriend?"

"The one who's coming to pick you up. I assume he's organized a snowplow or something?"

"Oh. Yes… that." My hand went to the back of my neck. "Well you see…" It occurred to me that I still had no idea why this man had come back. "What are you doing here anyway?"

"Oh. The phone didn't work. I thought I'd try ticking over the Copter again, but everything's dead."

"Copter? As in Helicopter?"

"Yes. The cold must have sapped the battery. Hell of a blizzard out there."

"Blizzard?" I was struggling to keep up with the conversation.

"Yes—thought I could fly over it." He laughed. "Proved me wrong! The Park was the only place I could land."

I held my hands up. "Wait, you landed a helicopter in the park outside the library. And there's a blizzard?"

He looked at me, face screwed up. "You didn't know?"

"Know what?"

"When was the last time you went outside?"

"This morning. I've been here all day. Why?"

He burst into sudden laughter. "Oh you are in for the shock of your life." He seized my hand and a shiver went up me; whether from his touch or the strange turn of the conversation, I didn't know. "Follow me."

He opened the library door. I followed.

There was a white glow at the end of the corridor. It had been snowing, I remembered that from when I drove to work this morning. But it couldn't have gotten that bad-

I stopped. "Well freeze my ears and call me an ice-block." The glass door at the front was a shoulder high wall of white, broken only by a narrow channel through the middle that was fast filling from above. "Is that… snow?"

"Afraid so."

I strode to the entrance, reaching for the door handle.

"I wouldn't-"

Too late, I heard his advice. As soon as I turned the knob, the door flung backward. Icy cold wind hit me like a hammer, knocking me off my feet. I yelped as I raised an arm to my face, protecting it from the snow that swirled around me, icy flakes stinging with the force of the blizzard that carried them.

A shadow leapt to my side, throwing its weight against the door until suddenly the noise and the wind stopped. It reached down to help me to my feet.

Gingerly I got up. *Nice move, dumbass.*

The stranger looked at me with concern. "Are you okay?"

I flushed. "Nothing hurt except my pride."

He laughed; a kind sound. "And that can be our secret if you want it to be."

My feet crunched on quickly melting snow as I moved to the door, this time pressing my face against the glass. Wind had piled a huge drift up against the door, but it still looked like more than two feet had fallen since this morning. "How can this be?"

"They're calling it the blizzard of the century. Highest snowfall recorded this year, and it's still falling. Or at least, that's what the reports said before I was forced to land."

His hand went to a ring on the index finger of his right hand. "I made a promise to someone. It was… well, it was worth the risk to keep it."

My heart melted, just a little. *What I wouldn't give to have a man like that.* "I'm sorry," I said. "For what it's worth."

"Well I might still make it, if I can get a lift with you?" The question hung in the air between us.

"Oh. That… Yes, well I didn't anticipate so much snow."

Maybe if I pretended for a while, I wouldn't have to actually admit that I didn't have a boyfriend— that it was all just a fantasy that lived in my head. "I don't think he's an option."

His hand went to his ring once more, rubbing it absently. "Damn."

"Perhaps we can walk out? You know, clear a way to a car?"

He walked to the doors, wiping a patch of frost with a well-tailored sleeve wide enough for us both to look through. "See out there?" He pointed at a shape in the gathering darkness.

"Is that… your helicopter?"

He nodded. "We don't want to be out at night in this, trust me. We wouldn't last five minutes."

"So… we wait out the storm?"

"I guess so."

This was happening faster than even my imagination could have moved. *Wait out the storm? We were spending the night together.*

CHAPTER TWO

"I'm Booker." He held out his hand.

"Clara." I giggled, hating myself even as I did it. Giggling? Seriously? Who giggled these days? *I did apparently—at least when I got nervous.* I reached out and took his hand tentatively, much more aware of how warm and real it was, now that I knew we were stuck here together. "Um, pleased to meet you." We stood by the counter in awkward silence for several moments.

"I guess we're spending the night together."

In my mind I ripped all my clothes off, growling like a cheetah. In reality, I raised an eyebrow. "Just as long as you don't get any funny ideas."

He raised his own eyebrow in return. "Such as?"

Ripping all my clothes off. Throwing me against a bookcase and making love to me. Anything you want.

"I've seen Day after Tomorrow. We will not be burning books if it gets cold."

He let out a laugh, then reached out to place his hand on my arm. "A librarian with a sense of humor—I like that."

I pulled away more sharply than I'd intended. "Yes. Well you can like, but you can't touch. That's the rules."

His hand fell. "Sorry, my bad. Your boyfriend, of course."

It would be better if I didn't correct him. I stayed silent.

"So," his gaze swept around the library as he popped himself onto the counter, "anything I should know?"

I winced. "Well you're not allowed to sit on countertops, for a start. Totally against library regulations."

He grinned, making no move to get down. "Do you always follow the rules?"

"Yes." I crossed my arms. "Now do you mind? You're breaking about 20 of them right now."

He jumped down spritely. "Sure, sorry. I'm just... more of a free spirit, that's all." He clapped his hands together. "Okay, I guess our first priorities should be food and warmth. Any food around here?"

I shook my head. "Regulations—no food on premises."

"Okay..." he said, thinking. "How about water fountains?"

I shook my head again and his hand went to the back of his neck. "I guess we can always melt snow if we have to." He raised an eyebrow at me. "Not that I'm allowed to burn any books to melt it."

Was he playing with me? I wasn't sure, but I shot him a look just in case. "Very funny, Mister."

He laughed. "Just joking. But it's going to get really cold if the central heating gives out. Do we have any fire blankets? Newspapers?"

I brightened. "Actually, I might have something better." I disappeared under the counter, returning awkwardly with a huge box labelled *Lost Property* on one side.

He reached across, taking the weight with ease. "What do we have here?"

"The box that time forgot," I said. "Put it on the ground, let's see what we can find."

He placed the box as directed, then sat beside it, rifling through the contents. I joined him.

"Hey, check it out!" he said, laughing. He pulled out a hot pink scarf and wrapped it around his neck. "What do you think, my color?"

I stifled a giggle. "Suits your skin tone. What else is there? I haven't looked for a while."

He quickly began to pull items out of the box. "Teddy bear, non-library book, car keys… wait, how the hell did this person get home?"

Now I really did burst out laughing. "I've got this sudden mental picture of someone driving a car Fred Flintstone style, with their feet hanging out the bottom."

Booker laughed but then stopped suddenly, his eyes alighting on an object he had spied. He snatched it up with a grin. "I think this is for you, ma'am." He pulled out a plastic bag that contained goggles and a teeny, tiny swimming costume.

I picked up the goggles, dangling them off one finger. "I'll wear these if you wear the costume?"

He laughed. "Sorry, it's a matching set. That would be cheating."

"Oh really?" I said, seizing the box and dragging it toward me. I fished inside quickly. "Well then this, sir, is for you!" With a flourish, I presented him a plastic tiara.

He placed it on his head and then posed. "What do you think?"

"Very handsome!"

"It's just a shame there is no matching wand," he said, pulling a sad face. "Because if I had one, maybe I could magic up…" He fished inside the box blindly. "This!"

I cocked my head to the side, observing the plain white top he'd pulled out. "Really? That's the best you could come up with?"

"Hmm… that was disappointing. I was hoping for something better." He threw it toward me.

I held it against my body and then laughed. The fabric was thin, with a plunging neckline. "Only disappointing if I don't try it on—my boobs would look great in this!"

His head snapped up. "Did I hear that right?"

"Sorry. The inner voice just slipped out. It does that sometimes."

"Any chance you'd model it anyway?"

I flushed bright pink. "Let's keep looking Mister. It's cold out, remember?"

He grinned, and suddenly my heart went all aflutter. "I know. That's why I suggested it!"

* * *

Half an hour later we were both decked out in rejects from the lost property box.

Booker had dressed me in mismatched gloves, a cowboy hat and the type of sweater everyone receives from their grandma at least once in their life. I couldn't really blame that last item for being left at the library.

I'd dressed Booker in a pink scarf, black leather purse, orange sarong and leg warmers. He'd worn it all with good humor, even the 'I'm with stupid' t-shirt that had an arrow pointing straight down. I wasn't sure how warm it would make us, but it sure had been a fun way to pass the time.

"Maybe we leave this stuff here until we get cold enough to use it," Booker said once we'd reached the end of the box. He stepped behind a bookshelf again to change.

"Ah… sure. Great idea," I said. The books didn't reach to the top of each shelf, and I was catching glimpses of flesh in jagged little outlines. His stomach was flat, I could tell that much. But was that a hint of abs? I craned surreptitiously to one side, where a low squat dictionary gave a slightly better view. *Uh huh. Definitely Abs.* That was his belly button for sure, and there was the trail of hair that led down-

The peep show ended as a shirt slid down and then moments later, he walked out. "You okay?" he asked, looking at me concerned. "You've gone all red."

I coughed. "Must be the central heating."

He shrugged. "I guess we shouldn't complain." His stomach growled, hand going to what I knew now to be rock hard abs. "I don't mind telling you, I'm beginning to get hungry."

My mind started to play out that t-shirt scene again. I squashed it down firmly. "Ah... sure. Me too."

"They say that you can get by without food for something like 30 days, but everyone needs to drink water or they'll die."

Now I nodded, focus entirely back on the conversation. I'd read the same in a book within these very walls.

He stood up. "Do you have any buckets around here? Let's get some of that snow inside so it can start melting."

* * *

We were almost at the outer doors when Booker stopped. "Wait. Is that... a café?" he asked, looking toward the community eatery on our left—one side of the corridor's windows looked in on it. "Why the hell aren't we eating there?"

He leaned his face up against the window. "Food, drink, *cakes*. We have to get inside!"

I motioned to the locked door behind us. "We don't have a key."

Booker glanced to the door, then back to the food inside. Then back to the door again. "I think I know where the key is. Wait here."

He ducked outside to a blast of cold air that swooped down the hallway like a ghost on a mission, returning 30

seconds later covered in white. A large rock the size of his
fist was clutched in strong fingers.

"Wait! You can't do that!"

His arm paused. "Yes I can. Have rock, will throw." He
gestured like a caveman as he spoke. "I'm sure when we
explain the situation-"

"Absolutely not." I cut him off. "We *are not* savages."

"But-"

"NO!"

He threw his hands up in the air. "Well what do you
suggest? That we starve?"

I sniffed. "That still doesn't mean you can steal. Society
has rules for a reason."

"What if I pay for it then?"

It took a moment to work out what he was talking
about. "The food?"

"Yes. And any damage I cause. I'm… not a poor man.
I'll pay for the window *and* make a sizeable donation.
Sound fair?"

I thought briefly. "I guess so."

"Good. It's settled." Then he winked at me. "Are you
going to help?"

I pulled back. "Me? I've never done anything like that
before."

"I don't make a habit of breaking and entering either,
trust me."

"No, I mean, something I'm not allowed to do."

"What, ever? You've never broken a rule?"

*Not in three years. Not since I broke the only one that mattered.
Not since I paid the price.*

I threw up my hands. "I work in a library, I enforce the
rules!" I forced a laugh. "I'm the bitch that tells everyone
else to be quiet!"

Gently, he pulled me to him. To the window. "It's time
to change that." He placed the rock in my hand.

"I don't know if I can do it." I looked at him. "Can I?"

"I told you, I'll pay the damages and more besides."

I hesitated. "What do I do?"

"Well, I'd suggest you back up a step or two, then throw it as hard as you can."

I hefted the rock once. Twice.

I could do this. It had been long enough, hadn't it?

Before I could think myself out of it, I pulled back to throw.

"Wait!" His hand seized my arm before I could launch the missile. He moved behind me, body pressing against mine, readjusting my trajectory. "Aim for the corner. Then we can reach through and undo the latch."

I took a couple of short, sharp breaths; his cologne on my tongue, his body giving me encouragement. *I could do this.*

I threw the rock as hard as I could. The window shattered with a crash.

I let out a whoop as I saw the glass tinkle down around me. "My heavens! I can't believe I just did that." I turned to him, eyes wide. I was flying. I'd been freed. "That felt goooood. Let's do it again!" I searched around for something else to throw.

His hands went to my shoulders with a chuckle. "Easy now Clara. No need to get overzealous, one's enough." He looked me in the eyes. "You've never really done anything like this before?"

I shook my head, eyes wide. Then, for no reason I could discern, I felt myself start to shiver. Tears began to well. "Not in a long time."

"Easy now." He pulled me into a hug. "That's the adrenaline starting to wear off. I'm sorry, it's my fault. I should never have let you get so worked up about this. If I had known…"

I shook my head. *How could he have known?*

"You just looked so damn happy, that's all."

I burst into tears. He held me tight until I was finished.

Son of a gun, I was being such an idiot. *Pull yourself together Clara!*

I took a deep breath, then pulled away. 'I'm sorry. You must think I'm crazy.'

"Not crazy, just cute. I've never met anyone like you Clara. Such a tough exterior, but so different on the inside." Hands moved gently to brush my hair back. "I'd like to see more of that. I'd like-"

I stiffened beneath him. *I'd shown too much already. I couldn't let myself get hurt again.*

His voice faltered. "It doesn't matter. I'm sorry." His hands clapped together. "You hungry? Because I'm buying."

CHAPTER THREE

"What now?" We sat at a cafeteria table amidst a pile of wrappers, our evening repast haphazard, but satisfying.

Booker twisted to look out the café windows. "I was actually thinking I might give the helicopter another crack."

It was still blowing a blizzard outside. "You're not planning on flying out in this weather, are you?" The thought formed an instant ball of tension in the pit of my stomach.

Booker shook his head. "No, no chance of that. But if the phones are still down, the helicopter radio is our best bet at getting in touch with the outside world. Not..." he looked hesitant. "Not that I want this night to end." Then he sighed. "But I figure you can call your boyfriend, tell him you're safe, and I can call... well, I have a couple of things I need to organize too."

Oh yes. *He still thought I had a boyfriend.* "Um. I wouldn't be too worried about things from my end. But... can I help you in any way?"

He shook his head, a strange expression flitting across his face, before he stood and walked to the counter. "Thanks, but not really I'm afraid. Even if that lost property box did have something warmer in it, it's really a one man job. I should be fine inside the helicopter. "

"So, I guess… I'll see you soon?"

He nodded, moving toward the door.

"Wait!" I ran back to the library proper, fishing under the main desk. "Here. Take this."

He took the large industrial flashlight I proffered, gratefully. "Thank you—see you soon."

Another blast of cold air, then he disappeared into the night.

* * *

It was while looking for a broom to clean up that I saw the note Booker had left beside the till.

> *Sincere apologies for the damage. This is for the food, hopefully the check covers the window. Keep the change.*
> *B*

Underneath lay several hundred dollars and a check for… I looked again. Good grief—$100,000! That was more than the entire building was worth! Who was this man that had walked into the library? I'd known he was wealthy—the helicopter kind of gave it away, but still!

I'd like him even if he didn't have money. Not that it matters— the only reason he's here is because of a freak storm. Guys like that don't go for girls like me. Better that I stick to my rules. Better that I stay away. Better that I let him continue to think I have a boyfriend.

I caught sight of the shattered window.

Then again, hadn't I just proved that some rules could be broken? That sometimes it was for the best?

I thought about that other rule I'd broken, oh so many years ago. And suddenly I knew it wasn't time. Not yet.

How do you think it's going to end Clara? All sunshine and rainbows? You're an overweight librarian who hasn't had someone even look at them in so long you can't remember. Life isn't a fairytale, and the pot at the end of the rainbow is full of something, but it ain't gold.

I dumped the glass in the bin and stalked from the cafe. I needed to change location. I needed to get back to the security of my books.

CHAPTER FOUR

I pottered for a while, doing jobs that I would normally do during business hours. But my mind kept coming back to Booker. To that offhand grin; the way he'd just walked into my quiet oasis and literally destroyed it.

I found myself smiling. Smiling at his participation in my goofy dress up game. Smiling at the memory of the window shattering. Smiling at the way he had held me after, and just let me cry until I got it all out. He still didn't know what that had meant to me—that acceptance for who I was. And I'd probably never tell him. But in my mind, I was grateful.

I picked up a book and walked down to the back shelf, sitting in my familiar aisle. It shouldn't have been comfortable, leaning with my back against a wall, surrounded by books. But it was—it was my one tiny little safe haven, more familiar than my room, with more happy memories to boot, too.

It was, I realized, the very aisle that Booker had gotten changed in. Another pleasant memory to associate with my corner. I thought about that again, those glimpses of flesh from between the bookshelves. Those hard, ripped abs. I wondered what his chest had looked like? I was allowed to imagine those things, wasn't I?

In my mind, I was safe. I couldn't be hurt.

If I closed my eyes I could see it now. See him taking off his shirt, button by button. His fingers deftly popping first one, then the other, starting at the top… no, starting at the bottom, revealing tantalizing glimpse after tantalizing glimpse of smooth, creamy flesh.

I'd be there of course. Right where I was now. He'd be undressing just for me.

The shirt fell to the floor with a smooth swish. "I want you so bad Clara."

"I want you too."

His pants followed next; a sexy striptease, the belt popping with a click. I could hear the zip as it was drawn downwards. I could see the thin trail of hair that led from his stomach to white Calvin Klein boxers. The pants fell to the floor with a swish, too.

"Do you like that?"

I nodded, eyeing the straining bulk hinted at so perfectly behind the white cloth. It was straining toward me. Just for me.

My hand slipped between my legs. It was warm down there. Warm for him.

"That's it baby. That's what I like. Just save some for me."

I began to circle gently. It felt good, after so long— after so much frustration and built up tension. My fingers caressed smooth cotton, and then when that wasn't enough, slipped under to touch bare skin. A shiver ran though me, a shiver at what I was doing right here on the library floor. Here I could be me. Here I could be liberated.

I gasped. Here I could be pleasured. My fingers flicked up to my mouth. I licked them slowly, thoroughly, then took them back down. Oh yes. I wouldn't have to lick them again, not at the rate I was going. I dipped them downward, running them gently around my edges, wetting them. Wetting me. I began to circle faster, thinking about Booker. About what he would do to me.

That was it. I could feel something inside me start to glow, moving slowly from the warmth I was generating between my legs to spread throughout my body. The warmth was building slowly in my pelvis too, a spinning, whirring center of pleasure that only moments ago had been pleasing, tingling; but now was something else. Something that made me catch my breath and circle even faster. I dipped my hands down again, and then again, pressing in deeper, imagining Booker inside me.

What I wouldn't give to have him in me right now. I could imagine him thrusting as my fingers reached their final furious crescendo, stoking the warmth into a fire that must explode at any moment inside of me.

He'd call my name as I came. As we came together; as he exploded inside me even as I did too.

I drew in a shuddering breath. I couldn't hold it in.
I could hear him calling it right now. "Clara! Clara!"

"Clara!" The voice intruding into my fantasy from the front of the library tipped me over the edge, even as my eyes opened and I realized it was real. Oh God. Oh God!

I squeezed my eyes shut, legs clenched around my fingers as I convulsed silently on the library floor, struggling not to scream from the pleasure that was exploding within me.

My body was on fire!
He was in the library, what was I doing?
"Clara! Are you there?"

I tried to answer but it came out in a squeak. I tried again. "Down… down the back," I called hoarsely. "Wait there, I'll come to you."

I stood, as quick as I was able, leaning against a bookshelf until I could stand by myself.

"Son of a biscuit" I whispered. *That had been a good one.* I moved, shakily, patting my hair and then, after looking down, smoothing my dress too. I took a deep breath, cleared my throat, and walked briskly toward the front counter, and the unknowing man who had only moments before taken me to pleasures unrivalled.

CHAPTER FIVE

"Are you sure you're okay? You look flushed."

I cleared my throat. "Just working hard in the back room." I changed the subject quickly. "How did the helicopter go?"

A hand went to the back of his neck. "Battery's gone because of the cold; no luck there."

"I've never been in a helicopter, did you know that?"

"Really?" Booker raised an eyebrow. "Well then madam, when we get out of here, allow me the honor of giving you your first flight."

Lot of first's happening tonight. "It would be my pleas-"

The library went black—so dark I couldn't see my hands before me. *I screamed.*

Booker's hands flew to mine, holding me, telling me it would be alright. His torch flicked on. "You okay?"

I nodded, thankful it was still too dark to tell the color of my face.

"I was afraid of this."

"What? Why are the lights out?"

"The storm. Only a matter of time until a tree hit a power line. Come on, let's pull back these curtains, see if we can't get a bit of light in here."

Windows rimmed the library building—long thin horizontal things built high above the shelves, curtained and accessible by low cords hung in spaced increments between them. We pulled each back one by one, travelling together across the library, and gradually the space was flooded with little sparkles and glimmers; the moon fighting hard to pierce the storm which raged outside.

I'd never been in the library like this; like another world, a wasteland where shadows played around corners, where the endless books lining shelf after shelf looked like the ribs of a great beast. It had an otherworldly quality, like anything could happen. Instinctively, I moved closer to Booker.

Our hands touched, fingers entwining before I could think about it. He was warm beside me—his grip an anchor within the ghost land we had created. I'd met him such a short time ago, but already I looked to him for food, for safety. *For pleasure.*

I shivered.

"So, ah, what's there to do around here at night?" Booker asked. He looked as shaken by our sudden contact as I was. Our hands parted. "I need to do something, to… take my mind off things."

"Well. It's a library after all," I said, the memory of his touch still warm in my mind. "My favorite is the romance section." *Lame Clara. Totally lame.*

Booker's hands went to his neck. "I was kind of thinking more like a board game or something. Romance really isn't my thing."

"Oh." *Not his thing?* "Well there's a small section. Fancy a game of Connect Four?"

We were on our third game— the decider—when I voiced the question that was on my mind. "Booker? What did you mean when you said romance wasn't your thing?"

He paused, hand hovering above the game before eventually slotting his disk.

"Can I tell you a secret?" he asked. "A dirty little secret I haven't told anyone?"

I looked at him apprehensively.

He beckoned me closer. "I've never been much of a library kind of guy."

"What do you mean?"

He sat back. "I've never really enjoyed books. They bore me – why read it when you can wait for the movie to come out?"

"You're not serious," I said, scandalized. "You're not seriously saying that to a librarian. *In her own library?*"

"I'll read the *Financial Times* for my job, and I have a passion for conservation projects, so I'll read that stuff occasionally too, but fiction just isn't my thing." He shrugged. "Romance is the worst. It's so boring! All that malarkey about true love and soul mates? It's just never sat true."

"You're joking, right?"

He shrugged. "Sorry."

I stood. "All right, you're on."

"What do you mean?" he asked, standing as well.

I spread my arms. "We're in no better place to prove you wrong, and we've got all the time in the world. We're going to find a book —a romance, in fact—that grabs you so much you want to read it right here, cover to cover."

"Now?"

I looked down at our game. "Would you rather I beat you at Connect Four again?"

"You haven't beaten me. This is the decider."

I bent down to slot a piece swiftly. It landed with a clink.

"Oh." His lips quirked at the corners. "Point made. All right then, what are the rules?"

I thought for a moment. "I have until dawn… and the bet can only be cancelled by mutual arrangement." I narrowed my eyes. "So that means no pulling out if you start to get bored!"

He shook my hand. "You're on. Okay, if you can find a romance that I genuinely want to read, dinner's on me when we get out. Five Star, all the way."

"Five Star?" I said, impressed. "Whatever it takes, I'm going to win this bet—even if it means resorting to violence." I looked at him, a smile creeping across my lips. "How do you feel about being beaten into submission with really thick encyclopedias?"

He chuckled. "I'm more the Alpha type than the submissive. But if you were doing the beating… well, maybe I'd make an exception."

Oh. Suddenly I was grateful for the torchlight casting shadows over my face.

I cleared my throat. "And… what do you want?" My voice was a whisper. "If you win?"

He looked at me speculatively, hand reaching for my cheek. "How about you…" He faltered, then his hand dropped. "Romance isn't my thing, Clara. You won't win."

Why did it feel like he'd wanted to say something else? "How about I cook you dinner then?" I suggested.

He nodded, lips pressed tight.

I hesitated, but then decided to charge on. "Come on, I already know the first book I want to show you."

We stopped at a shelf toward the start of the fiction section. "*Pride and Prejudice.* One of the greatest love stories of all time." I knew this wouldn't be his final choice, but I was prepping him for something.

He took the book from me, reading the back briefly, then returned it. "Nope, too boring, not enough action. You're going to have to do better than that."

I walked swiftly to another shelf, playing my trump card. "Then how about this!"

"*Pride and Prejudice… and Zombies*?" Booker looked up in confusion.

"I told you I'd do anything to win this bet. Even if it means having you read the boy version of one of the greatest books ever written." I leaned toward him, hand to the side of my mouth. "Plot spoiler, there's ninjas as well."

He began to flick through it. "This is actually a thing?"

I nodded. "So? Do I win the bet?" I asked.

"Do they still live happily ever after?"

"Of course."

He turned away. "Then it's a fantasy, not a romance."

This time the silence was pregnant with confusion. "Why would you say that?" I asked.

"It's a long story."

"We've got all night."

He opened his mouth, then closed it, pain behind his eyes. "It would bring the mood down. Show me something else—I'm enjoying myself, regardless of how it looks."

I thought for a moment. "What about *Sugarbabe*? It's got lots and lots of sex?"

He raised an eyebrow. "Trying to turn me on? Keep it up and the dinner you're cooking will be done in Lingerie."

I slapped him on the shoulder. "That's not fair!"

"Hey. I don't make the rules, I just enforce them."

Booker was a mystery. He was so sexual—I'd never met a man who could make me blush so easily. But there was romance in him too, regardless of what he said. I could tell it in the way he'd held me in the café. The way his hand had found mine in the dark. What did he read?

An idea occurred and suddenly I was scampering though familiar aisles to another corner, Booker following with a bemused expression on his face.

I twirled, an excited look in my eyes. "Presenting a tale about sex and love, with all the saucy bits left in."

"Casanova?" he asked, reading the title. "That guy from Italy?"

"Just hear me out," I said, hands raised. "Yes, it's about a man that lived 400 years ago. But I think you'll find him a kindred spirit. He's the ultimate romantic, though he protests it furiously. Every woman he ever meets falls for him: he's handsome, intelligent and the most delightful charming rogue you could ever hope to meet."

"Kindred spirit. Do... you think those things about me?"

I looked away, blushing furiously. "That's not what I meant."

"What did you mean then?"

Word's failed me temporarily. I stomped my foot. "Look, do you like the book or not?"

His hands lingered on the spine. Then he gave it back. "Not for me. I'll probably get it out someday soon—if only because it will give me the chance to see you again— but it doesn't make me want to sit down on the floor and begin reading right now."

I growled. "You're not playing fair!"

He flashed a smile. "You're pretty when you're angry. It brings out those cute dimples. Ready to give up yet?"

I shook my head, reassessing the man before me. What was my attraction to him? And why was it so important to prove that he could enjoy a romance, if only he found the right one?

My fingers started to drift along the cold shelves, heading to a very particular aisle before I'd even realized what I was doing.

When I'd first started working for the library, I'd discovered a collection of books that...well, that had been purchased in a freer age, or perhaps by mistake. They weren't the sort of books you normally found in a library. They weren't the sort of romance the good citizens of this town normally read. But I'd read them. Every single one. And I'd found a freedom in them I'd never known in real life. Perhaps this was a romance he could enjoy. A romance we could both lose ourselves in. *What did I have to lose?*

I arrived at the reference section, the part that abutted the back wall. My hands paused on a large, thick tome.

"Chemistry 101?" Booker asked. "Look, no offense but if you think that's going to interest me-"

I pulled it out, then reached into the space behind. There'd been an old shelf here before these stacks were put up, built into the very wall. It was now my own secret little storage place; a receptacle for 101 dark, debaucherous fantasies. I pulled a slim volume from its hiding place. The torch illuminated a scantily clad woman below the words *Deflowering Daisy*.

"Oh," Booker said, startled. He opened a page at random. "Wow. It's chemistry all right, but not what I was expecting." He lowered the book to look in my eyes. "Is this yours? Is this... what you read?"

I avoided his gaze. "Sometimes. I kind of found it one day and couldn't stop reading. It's another world, you know? Where people do what they think about, not what the rules say they have to."

A glimmer of understanding sparked behind his yes. "And, you always follow the rules, don't you?" He moved closer. "Is... this," his hands gestured to the page, "is this what you think about? What you dream of in your head?"

How could he read me so easily? Like one of my books, plucked right off the shelf. It scared me.

"You will too, after you read it," I said, taking the conversation in a different direction. "It's my secret weapon. The thing I'm going to use to win this bet." I placed the torch on a shelf, where it would illuminate the aisle. "I dare you to read one scene and not want to keep reading until the very last page."

He began to read. The perpetual half smile he usually held on his face disappeared, replaced first by furrowed brow, then a quick lick of his lips as he glanced up at me. "This is really... umm... descriptive."

"I know."

"I like it," he said.

I glanced down to his jeans. "I can tell."

He shifted uncomfortably. "I won't lie. It's kind of turning me on. Is that allowed in a library?" He turned to me, his next question layered with meaning. "Is it something you would allow?"

Inside, my inner voice was doing little cartwheels. This was what I'd been waiting for! The man of my dreams was standing before me with a hard-on that would make a stallion proud, asking me how I felt about him being turned on. I wasn't stupid. I could see where this was leading.

I shook my head. It was still too soon. Three years, and the hurt was just too much. It wasn't something I could just forget about. It wasn't something I could just get over.

How could I ever? I was the one that broke the rules! I only had myself to blame for the pain that followed, and I wasn't going to go through that again.

"I'm sorry," I said, stepping backward. "I got caught up in the moment. I… I should never have shown you those books. I didn't mean to mislead you."

His hand reached out to me, wiping away a tear. "I don't understand."

I shook my head. "I never used to be like this. I used to be… different. But I'm not that person anymore."

"What happened?"

"I don't want to talk about it."

"We all have our secrets. Tell me yours."

I shook my head. "It was a silly idea."

"I'll start," he whispered. "When I first walked into this library, I was having the worst day in the world. You couldn't imagine. But that changed as soon as I met you."

His hand caught mine. "You're funny, and though you play at the strict librarian, you don't fool me. I can see a softer side underneath. So different to what I am normally attracted to. This night with you—the break-in, the clothes box—it's been so refreshing!"

His hand squeezed mine gently. "And so here's my secret. I'm… attracted to you. I want you. And I've been trying hard all night to stay away because you've got a boyfriend, but I can't."

He turned away from me. "I'm sorry. I should never have said anything."

I was so stunned I said the first thing that came to mind. "What boyfriend?"

"Your boyfriend. The footballer." His hand went to the back of his neck. "God, I'm such a fool. The last thing I would want to do is cause trouble between you two."

"There is no boyfriend," I whispered.

"What?"

"I made him up."

"No boyfriend?" he asked. He spun back, a spark of hope on his face.

I nodded.

"Then… I can do this?" He leaned in, gently, toward me, to kiss me tentatively on the lips with the barest of brushes.

It was like a butterfly's touch—one that left you just hoping, *wishing*, for it to come back and alight properly.

My lips parted. His hand came to the back of my head. And then he was kissing me with a fire such that I'd never experienced before. Passionate, tender and so full of longing and promise that I came gasping back up for air and then dove straight back down, like a woman drowning in a sea of desire.

It felt so good. It felt so right. My hand went to his neck and then his broad, strong back; feeling the musculature beneath his shirt, fighting the desire to rip it off him. I gave in, fingers fumbling for buttons as his did the same to my dress; running his hands over my curves with a moan, seeking out the means with which I might be freed.

It was different this time. Different to the last. Finally, I'd found someone worth breaking the rules for.

All these years, I kept my promise. Now I'm breaking it with a man whose last name I don't even know.

My lips froze. It was true. *I didn't know his last name.*

Suddenly a wave of fear swept through me. Fear that it would end like last time. Fear, and horror, and… and shame.

I pulled away. "I'm sorry. I can't."

Booker's hands went to my shoulders, his body trembling with desire. But then he saw my face and suddenly his eyes held only concern. "Clara? What's wrong?"

"I can't. The last time this happened… well, I made a promise to myself that it would never happen again."

"But it feels so right!"

"So did last time."

His hands gently cupped my face. "Tell me Clara. Whoever it was—he can't hurt you now."

I shook my head. *How could I tell him he had it all wrong? That I had been the one at fault?* "I don't do one night stands. I don't have relationships at work. I won't give someone my heart, ever again."

He looked at me softly. "You really feel that way?"

It still felt like yesterday—that moment, three years ago, when the man I'd thought I was beginning a new life with had laughed in my face. He'd said marriage was a contract, and if I'd broken it, why should he keep his promises?

He'd been right. I didn't deserve love. Not after what I'd done.

I shook my head sadly. "It's the rules." *Keeping them was my penance.*

Booker's hand gently brushed a strand of hair behind my ear. "Rules have their place, yes. They protect us; they stop us from making mistakes over and over again."

It was like he had read my mind. I nodded, tears welling.

His eyes locked with mine. "But here's the thing. Sometimes rules grow outdated too. We grow up, and move on, and no longer need them. When that happens, keeping them becomes the mistake."

"I can't risk it. Not again."

"With the right guide, you can walk a new path. With a connection this strong, some rules are meant to be broken." He kissed me gently. "Let me be that guide. Let's explore that connection."

I wanted to believe him. I really did. I'd been unhappy for so long. But even if I didn't like the woman I had become, could I change?

The cage was sealed too tight. "I'm sorry," I said, turning away. "I can't. It was stupid to think I ever could."

"Clara!" Booker called softly.

I shook my head. "It's over, okay?" I gestured around us. "Make a pile—we'll burn books to keep warm, starting with the one in your hand."

There was silence as I left the stack. Silence as I made my way to the front of the library.

Then I heard a voice.

"Wait!" Booker came running after me; his face, desperate, wild. "Wait. The competition isn't over yet, is it?"

I turned. "You win, okay? I don't want to find you another book. I don't want to play this game." I started walking again.

"So you're going to break your own rule? I thought we had till dawn."

I stopped, still not facing him. "That's not fair."

"I know. But I'm doing it anyway."

I spun. "Well then I'm just not going to find another book! There was never any rule that said I had a quota to meet."

He walked toward me. "What if I find a book?" he asked. "The rules were never just about you. They were about us. We had to find the romance together." He looked at me, a mischievous twinkle in his eyes. "You're not a rule breaker, are you?"

I shook my head, furious and impressed at his logic all at the same time.

"Well then come on. I've got one last thing I want us to try. But you're going to have to help me—you're the librarian, after all."

He took my hand and now it was his turn to pull me toward the stacks. "I guess I'm looking for your reference section. Social Sciences? No wait. Probably Physiology. Something like that."

Despite myself, I was curious. Who was this man pulling me through my own library? Who was this man that could take my tears, and make them disappear as if they had never been?

"Here we are." His fingers trailed dusty, disused spines until they stopped on a large, thick book wrapped in nondescript green leather.

I pulled it from the shelf, knowing the title before I had even seen it.

"The Kamasutra," he said, turning toward me. "A romance I can read. A book of rules you can follow."

CHAPTER SIX

Could I do *it? Could I forgive that girl from three years ago?* I wanted to be happy. So desperately.

Booker drew me to him. I knew I should protest, should pull back, but suddenly I didn't want to. My inner voice needed this. My body needed it too. The memory of his kiss on my lips was still too fresh. The vision of him as I pleased myself too real.

But still I protested. "I can't Booker. I can-"

He cut me off with a kiss. Forceful, passionate, full of everything he could have said but hadn't, full of everything I had ever gone without. "It's the rules Clara. You have to."

His lips moved over my cheek to graze against my ear, then move down to the hollow where my neck met my shoulder. "You see, I've discovered your weakness. You're mine, now."

I moaned as his lips sent goosebumps flying in little shivers all over my body. *Could I do this? Could I follow the rules I myself had set? If I followed them for bad, could I now follow them for good?*

My body arched as his hands ran down my back. They were strong hands; safe arms. This could be different from last time.

"I did agree to do whatever it takes," I whispered. I seized his head and brought him back to my mouth, kissing him with all the hunger of ten years lost. He was salty on my lips, his cheeks lightly stubbled. We stood in the library, clutching each other, hands exploring each other's bodies, mouth's exploring each other's souls. Hands went for the second time to his shirt, unbuttoning it with a haste born of fear that I might stop myself before it was complete. I was three buttons down before I tore the rest, wrenching it open with a ripping sound that sent matching shivers up my fingers.

Oh yes. Hairless chest rippling with slabs of muscle – not overdone, just perfectly formed and defined. Abs that washed down his stomach like river stones on a stream of tanned skin; a trail of hair that started at the waist, inching down to hidden pleasures below. It was better than I'd imagined, better than the glimpses between the bookshelves.

His fingers hooked under the straps of my dress as I drank him in, his eyes eager to explore my body. But I wouldn't have that. Not yet. There was too much I wanted to explore of him, first.

"Uh uh," I said, stepping away. I was panting. "If we do this, we have to follow the rules."

"Fuck the rules," he said, lunging for me.

I skipped away, finger wagging. "The rules are what got you here. Do you really want to deviate from them?"

His hand went to the back of his neck. "What do I have to do?" he said. "Just say the word."

I bent down to pick up the book he had dropped. "As I seem to remember, the deal was to find something that you wanted to read from start to finish." I held it out to him and winked. "We're going to act out what you're reading."

His eyes went wide as I dropped to my knees. I had a secret advantage here. The benefit of being a librarian. *I'd read the book already. I knew what was coming.*

He opened to the first page and began to read. "Mouth congress for him."

Slowly, I drew the zipper down on his suit pants. I left the belt done up.

I heard him swallow, loudly. "There are eight kinds of fellatio," he said, "each one is done right after the other."

I could see the bulk of him straining within. I ran my fingers lightly over the fabric covering it and heard his voice waver. It wanted to be freed. *I wanted to be freed.* I reached past the zipper, exploring the mound before me, caressing it gently with my fingers.

"Step 1: *The Nominal Congress.* She places the head of the... of the penis between her lips and moves it around."

I looked up at him, to find him reading, wide eyed, then returned to the task at hand. Gently, I drew the cotton of his boxers down. He sprang free, and I maneuvered his member outside the pants with a murmur of appreciation. He was beautiful—magnificent, hard and standing at attention entirely for me. Big, yes, but manageable, when it came time for that. I gazed at it, hypnotized, delighted at the part I had to play. I ran my hands up its length, then gently lowered my mouth to hover above it. Hot breath drifted over his skin as I breathed out, causing him to moan. Then slowly, delicately, I drew him between my lips; one hand around his base for support. I took only the tip, knowing what was yet to come. Knowing it would drive him wild.

"Step 2." He drew a deep breath as I rolled his head around my mouth. I could taste him, faintly, as his excitement grew.

"Step 2: Gently nibble the shaft of the penis."

My head pulled back, leisurely drawing myself off him, lips retaining contact until the very last second. Then I held him slightly to the side, head returning once more to alternately kiss then nibble the skin down one complete side of his shaft. I felt his legs waver against me. Shivers broke out on my skin as I heard him moan.

"Step 3: Take the semi-erect *lingam* with your lips and draw the foreskin back as it hardens."

I giggled, eyeing the rigid member before me. "I think you've beaten me to that one. Next!"

"Push the head-. Ooooh" He groaned as I anticipated his next words, slipping my lips over his member once more and starting to bob up and down, still just on his tip. "… into your mouth and then withdraw."

I could feel him in my mouth. Feel his passion, just for me. The way I could excite him—it was liberating.

"Now kiss it, as if you were kissing my lower lip, holding it in your hands," he read.

My hand began to slide up and down his shaft as the bobbing of my mouth stilled to focus on gentle suction. I imagined myself at his mouth, sucking his lower lip gently off his teeth. I could feel his thick, hard shaft between my hands, starting to throb with a tension that I was creating. I had thought it was hard before, but now it was swelling under my ministrations, growing even harder.

It felt so powerful. So hot. I wanted to take his whole shaft in my mouth, to own it completely, but I couldn't. Not yet. Just as he was bound by the rules, I realized I was too. The area between my own legs was growing warm, a tension fast building, built of the power I had over this man. The power these rules had over us both.

Booker groaned above me. "I don't know how much more of this I can take."

My head rose, though my hand kept going. "You can do it. What's the next step? Read it out."
"Step 6: *Rubbing*. Touch the penis all over with your tongue and mouth."

My hands stopped their friction, letting him go briefly to stand quivering in the air before me. "See, now we take it slower."

Slower indeed, even as my own blood began rushing faster. I couldn't take this, and I was the one dealing it! My right hand left him to travel down my own stomach. Pulling up the hem of my dress. Feeling my own warmth. I began to lick his shaft like an ice-cream. My right hand began to circle gently.

Oooh. "Doesn't that feel better?" I breathed.

He groaned in response.

I began to lick him faster, harder, moving in response to my own pleasures quickly building. I was spiking, sharp little peaks of pleasure rocketing me ever upwards to join him in excitement.

"Mmm." I was starting to lose concentration, the pleasure below making my pleasuring of him more and more difficult.

I passed my tongue over the end of him, licking the salty drops that were appearing there more quickly now. He didn't have long to go. But neither did I. "Keep going," I groaned. "Keep going."

"Step 7," he said, voice straining. "*Sucking a Mango Fruit.* Oh no. Oh, I don't think I can take this."

"Read it out," I breathed. I had started running my index finger in a line up and down myself now. That ball of tension was building again, growing within my hips and my heart, threatening to take over my world.

"Insert the top half of the penis into your mouth," he struggled, "and… and suck it."

I dove down onto him as my fingers dove into myself below, pleasuring us both with a force bordering on wild abandon. My head rode his long, thick length. First one then two fingers plunged in then out of myself, slippery and wet. I wanted this so bad, and I could taste him. Feel him.

"Oh God. I'm so close!" he whispered.

I prayed he was, for both our sakes.

"Step 8: *Swal... Swallowing Up*," he said, voice weak. "Put the whole penis into your mouth as if you're going to swallow it, press... pressing to the very end."

My hand went to his hips and then my mouth slid down deeper, deeper, deeper onto him, deeper than I had thought possible. My lips touched his base, gripping the shaft tightly, and then I slowly, slowly, slowly slid back up. He groaned, a sound of pure agonized pleasure. I felt him swell harder than I'd ever thought possible.

"Well done." I whispered as I came up off him. "Isn't this a book you want to read?"

"Fuck the book," Booker growled. He pulled me roughly to my feet, pressing me back against a book case with a force that sent a thrill through me. His eyes were clouded with lust. "I want you!"

He leaned in to kiss me, hard, on the lips. His hand went to my dress and then he was lifting it up, tearing at my underwear. My hands went to his head—turned on, aroused, just a little bit scared. What force of nature had I awakened within this man? What passions had I unleashed?

The cotton came away in his hands with an audible rip. I raised a leg to his hip and then he scooped me in his strong arms, my other leg raising to straddle his hips as he lifted me from the ground. My back pressed into the bookshelf.

He pressed into me.

It was everything I'd imagined, and yet somehow those fantasies paled in comparison, too. I felt each inch of his long, hard member as he slid into me; a thrill that grew with every inch, higher and higher.

I wrapped my arms around his neck, pressing myself into him. I couldn't take it. I couldn't hold on any longer. The thrill was spreading throughout my body, started by my own hand but finished by him. He began to move, plunging slowly but building quickly until he was thrusting over and over again. I gasped. The thrill exploded within me.

"Booker!"

He was veritably pounding me into the bookshelf behind. I groaned with each sweet movement; the feel of his body against mine, the thrill within me going on and on and on.

Books began to fall to the floor all around us. He let out an almighty groan, and then I felt him release inside me.

"Oh God!" His fingers curled through my hair and shockwaves flew through my body, zinging up through me, rebounding back down to double my own pleasure with each thrust inside; each book that flew from the shelves. My pleasure didn't stop until he had given everything he could and we both lay panting against the disheveled shelf behind.

* * *

I picked up the final book, the one that had started it all, to put it back on the shelf.

"You're such a librarian," Booker said, smiling.

I eyed him. "Should I leave it on the floor perhaps? That would just be anarchy."

He laughed. "You can't put it away just yet."

"Why not?"

He moved toward me. "I haven't finished reading, that's why."

My finger went to my lower lip. "Felt like you were finished to me."

He looked down, then back up at me, raising an eyebrow.

I followed his gaze. "Oh."

No he wasn't finished. Not by a long shot. "What now then?"

He pulled the book from my hands. "We keep reading. We do have till dawn, after all."

CHAPTER SEVEN

Communications came online around sunrise, signaled by a thousand discrete beeps as message after banked up message was received by our phones.

Booker had the majority, of course. I got two: one from my landlord asking why my rent was overdue, the other from Netflix asking if I'd like to upgrade my account.

We forced a path through the snow soon after; out through the corridor, past the café with its smashed window and $100,000 check, past a helicopter now visible only as a mound of white.

The night had been more than just sex. Though there had been a lot of that, so much that I blushed just thinking about it. There'd been a connection. Something primal and spiritual that joined us at the mind, as well as the hip. It had started, I think, when he'd first held me: that first time I'd broken a rule and shattered the window for food.

He was the one, I knew it. Such a short amount of time, and yet it already felt like forever. It was like suddenly I'd woken up to find a whole new world around me, the snow covering up my sins as well as the streets.

They were only ever sins in my mind. The man I'd been married to was happy now—another wife, and a beautiful child. And the man I'd left him for those three years ago no longer had a hold over me. *His words couldn't harm me anymore.*

The mistakes of the past didn't have to taint the future. Booker had taught me that. Falling in love didn't mean it would end in disaster. Breaking a marriage up once didn't mean I would do it again. I wasn't that same girl. It didn't have to have the same ending.

"Clara? Are you crying?"

I wiped at my eyes with a sleeve. "Sorry. It's the cold. Makes my eyes sting."

His arm went round my waist, enfolding me in a warm embrace from which I never wanted to leave. We stayed there, my head resting on his shoulder, until a car engine sounded in the distance.

"That'll be me," he said pulling away. A silver Porsche was approaching.

I'd forgotten he was wealthy; the Porsche just another reminder of the divide I'd have to deal with eventually. His wealth—or rather, my lack of it—hadn't mattered last night; we had both been equal under our blanket of snow. But how were we going to make this work in the light of day?

I could imagine him opening the door to whisk me away. *"Come with me,"* he'd whisper. *"My wealth is nothing. I'd give it all up for you."*

I'd shake my head with a laugh. "You fool," I'd whisper back. "I'm not asking you to." Then we'd drive away into the sunset and live happily-

I shook my head. The daydreams could end now. I'd finally found someone worth breaking my own rules for. I could be a new person. I could start a new life beside him.

The silver Porsche pulled up to the curb, the shadow of a thin blonde vaguely visible through the driver's side glass.

I reached for his hand, but he was worrying the ring on his right index finger. "You sure you'll be okay here?" he asked.

"I'll manage."

His hand went to the door. I leaned in for a kiss, but he pulled away. "I'm sorry," he said. "I'd better not."

"Why?" I asked, brow furrowing.

"Clara, last night everything seemed so simple. I thought I knew all the answers. But now… well, it's complicated."

Oh no. Please.

His hand went to the ring on his right hand again. He pulled it off, then slipped it onto his left. "I can explain-"

No no no no no.

"Who is it?" I said, voice rising. "Who's in the car?"

He looked at me, emotion a sudden storm across his features. He cleared his throat. "I'm sorry," he said. "It's my wife."

PART 2:

BY THE LETTER

There'd been something between us all night—the warmth of Booker's hands, the way he'd held me when I cried, the way his eyes went wide when I made that joke about my breasts.

Now, finally, I've found love again, and it's given me the strength to break the rules I created oh-so-long ago.

But daylight is coming.

And things always look different in the light.

CHAPTER ONE

The helicopter was gone—that was the first thing I noticed.

It was the first time I'd left the house in… well, when you start doing calculations based on the number of Chinese food containers left on the kitchen table, you don't need an exact number.

I'd fallen for a married man. *A man who, still glowing with the after effects of our passion, had slipped into the car beside his wife and driven off with a promise that he would call shortly.*

The girls had called saying he'd phoned, but I wanted nothing to do with him. It had only taken one night to break down my walls. Now they were so high that no man could ever come near me again.

But I'd healed enough to function—it was time to go back to work; the reason I was standing in the snow outside my library. My vacation days were about run out, and I was getting danged sick of Chinese food.

I took a deep breath and entered the outer door, the wind shutting off with a snap as it closed behind me. A long corridor lay ahead; the library at the other end, the community café that occupied the front of the building to my right. The window I had broken was fixed, that was good. I peered through it. There were renovations going on inside as well: plastic chairs, white walls and glass cabinets now replaced by a forest of green—some of it, actual forest. Potted trees graced the floor and tables. Ferns and vines hung from roof and walls. And in the far corner a huge mural of a tree was being constructed from recycled timber, the branches spreading out along walls and roof. Someone had propped a super cute stuffed toy monkey at its apex; a mascot surveying the café before it.

I squinted. There were books everywhere, too. The old beat up stainless steel counter had been cut at the front to become a bookshelf highlighting endangered species across the world. Plastic tables had been replaced with long, picnic style constructions with stacked books at each corner for legs. And the huge mural sported books hanging from its branches instead of fruit—food for the mind just waiting to be plucked.

The café was being renovated to fit its surroundings— the parkland outside, and the library next door. It was beautiful, but it must have cost a fortune.

At least he stayed true to his word. The thought came unbidden to my mind—I pushed it away. It was time to move on.

* * *

My co-worker Sandra came in at nine, when the library officially opened. I had a love / hate relationship with Sandra. She was tall, skinny and happily single—everything I was not. She squealed, rushing over to give me a huge hug before standing back to hop from foot to foot with excitement.

There was only one thing that could make Sandra wring her hands so. "Let me guess. You have news about a boy?"

She nodded energetically. If enthusiasm were raindrops, she'd be Lake Michigan.

"So that sexy librarian pic you put on Tinder worked?"

She nodded but then shook her head, confused. *Okay, so it had worked, but that wasn't the news.*

"You've been out on a second date with someone?"

She shook her head.

I sighed. "Ok, out with it then. Make me jealous."

She bit her lip. "Promise you won't be mad."

"You drive me crazy, but never mad. Go on, I promise."

"Well, have you seen the new foreman yet? From the café renovations?"

I shook my head. "This is my first day back, remember?"

"He's so dreamy!"

I laughed. "Sandra, you think everyone is dreamy."

She stuck out her tongue. "Whatever. Just wait till you see him—even you would get drunk in his eyes, little miss stone cold sober."

I loved Sandra, but I didn't want to talk about boys right now. "I'm really happy for you—you'll be great together."

Sandra was still hopping from side to side. "Wait! He doesn't want me. He got out half the romance books in the library!"

"Probably thought they were choose-your-own adventures."

She was literally jumping up and down now. "Stop interrupting. That's not the best part!"

I sighed. "Alright, out with it!"

"He asked what you read!" she squealed.

I looked at her properly for the first time. "What?"

The words came out in a tumble. "He came a week ago and asked what you read!"

I held my hands up. "Okay Sandra, from the beginning. What the heck are you talking about?"

"The cute foreman? He's been popping in every day since he started. We're all enormous fans, he's so dreamy-"

"Back on track Sandra. The books, remember?"

"Oh yes. He asked what your favorite books were. Said he'd been talking to you about romances."

"And?"

"And what?"

"What did you say?"

"We gave them to him, obviously. *Pride and Prejudice*, *Romeo and Juliet*—as many as we could find." Her perfect eyebrows waggled conspiratorially. "Romances, Clara. *That means he's romantic.*"

"You didn't think to call me first? Ask my permission?"

She rolled her eyes. "Would you have said yes?"

"Of course not!"

"Exactly."

This was just what I needed—another lovesick suitor. Three years alone and now that the door was open, it seemed everyone was knocking. *Time to shut it, hard.* "If you see him again, give him one final recommendation. Something that's a bit more realistic."

Her head cocked to the side; an inquisitive puppy.

"Tell him to read *Carrie*, by Stephen King. That should give him the right idea."

* * *

Sandra left me alone after that, but as I began to stack shelves my mind went back to another man, not so long ago, who had been interested in what I read. A man I'd shared one magical, terrible, wonderful night with in the library.

How would the story have played out if I hadn't walked him to his car?

We'd have pet names for each other, maybe. Cute little things that only we understood. I'd call him Mr. Lover, because he hated romances. He'd call me... I thought for a minute.

Sheets. Because they were great in a book and great on a bed. I giggled at that, letting the scene play out in my mind.

"Sheets! Baby. Put that book down and come give me a kiss."

"Now, now Mr. Lover, you know I'm still working." I'd put the books I was holding down anyway and fly into his arms. Sandra would be arching her eyebrows at us, but we wouldn't care. "You really have to stop coming to visit me at work, you know."

"You don't like being reminded of where it all began?" he'd ask. Then he'd pluck the Kamasutra from the shelf, and flick to a random page. "Let's see... what shall we try tonight?"

I'd laugh and snatch the book from his hand. "Get out of here, you. See you tomorrow."

He'd blow me a kiss then stride out the door; a gallant, magical prince about to get on his horse. Or maybe his Pegasus. He did own a helicopter, after all.

I scowled, thumping another book onto the shelf in front of me. Pegasus—how appropriate. A mythical horse for a make believe man.

CHAPTER TWO

I saw Booker at lunchtime.

He was sitting in a reading chair, legs flung casually over an armrest like he owned the place. He must have come in when I was in the stacks.

I strode straight to him. "What the heck are you doing here?"

His face lit up. "O Clara, my Clara! Wherefore art thou been my Clara?"

I stopped. *That was not what I'd expected to hear.* "Are you... quoting Shakespeare to me?"

He sat up straighter. "O, speak again, bright angel. For thou art as glorious to this day as is a winged messenger of heaven."

"That's... Romeo and Juliet."

He held up the book in his hands. "One of your favorite romances, I believe."

"Wait. It's you? The one that's been borrowing the books?"

He acknowledged my question with a dip of his head.

"But... why?"

"I want to know you, Clara—this mysterious, beautiful librarian who has stolen my heart." His arms spread wide, adopting Shakespearean speech once more. "My soul is made out of lead, and it's so heavy it keeps me stuck on the ground so I can't move."

He was charming, sitting here quoting verse in my library, I'd give him that. But I was angry, and I knew Shakespeare too. "Talk not to me, for I'll not speak a word," I snapped. "Do as thou wilt, for I have done with thee."

His face fell. "You really feel that way?"

I stared past him, afraid he'd see the tears in my eyes. "How could you? How could you do that to me?"

He stood. "Clara. That's why I'm here. I'm... I'm sorry."

I backed away. "No. You don't get to say that. You don't get to apologize. You're married, Booker. Married! You led me down the garden path, made me fall in love, and then literally left me for another woman."

"Clara. That's what I'm here to explain." His hand went to the back of his neck. "I know it seems bad… but, well, it's complicated."

I crossed my arms. "This is going to be good."

"It's like this. We're getting divorced."

My foot tapped until I realized that he had, in fact, said everything he wanted to say. "That's it, that's all you have to say? 'We're getting divorced?'"

"No… but hopefully it's a start. Clara… there's a pre-nup agreement, and we're separating, and it's nasty, and-"

"Stop," I said. "Just stop."

He paused, puppy dog eyes that did nothing but infuriate me further. Did he think being handsome was all it would take? Did he think a couple of platitudes about the future would be enough to sway me? I'd heard it all before. *Literally.* It was like I was reliving a conversation from three years ago.

Only this time, I knew how to answer. "That's not good enough," I said. "Answer me this. Are you still married?"

"Technically... yes."

"Then you cheated on her. With me. Marriage is a contract Booker, and if you've broken it why should I trust any other promise?"

"But-"

"My only love sprung from my only hate!" I said, cutting him off with verse. "Too early seen unknown, and known too late!"

He looked at me, helpless. "Clara. Please. Let's talk about this. I have so much I want to say."

I beckoned him closer. "You made a fatal error if you hope to impress me by reading Romeo and Juliet."

"I don't understand," he said. "I thought-"

I cut him off again, tears streaming down my face. "The characters love each other, yes. But in the end, Juliet still dies of a knife through the heart."

CHAPTER THREE

He was in the same chair, reading the same book, the following lunchtime.

I stormed up to him once more. "This is stalking. You need to leave!"

He raised an eyebrow. "Why? I'm overseeing the renovations next door, and last time I checked it was a free library. Are you going to tell me I'm not allowed inside?"

"You know what I mean. You're not welcome."

"Romeo said it best. 'I cannot bound a pitch above dull woe. Under love's heavy burden do I sink." He leaned forward. "Clara, I need to talk to you. To explain."

"Are you still married?"

"Well, yes."

"Then what is there to explain? It's over, Booker."

"Don't be like that Clara, please. That night in the snowstorm—it was something special, you know it."

"I thought I did. But I'll not be the third person, not again." I turned, storming away before he could see the tears in my eyes.

* * *

I began to dread the lunch hour. Every day for three weeks he came to sit in the same spot and read his romances. He didn't bother me, not after that first day. Just walked straight to his chair, sitting engrossed in his book until his time was up.

I also began to look forward to it. How could I hate someone so much, yet still covet that brief glance of tall, dark and handsome before I turned away with pointed cold shoulder?

It got to the stage where I even sent Sandra to chat to him. She was better looking than me; she was also a lot more his type. *If she could catch his attention…*

It didn't work. She reported with annoyance that he'd spent more time asking how I was, than anything else.

It didn't matter that he was clearly still interested. It didn't matter that reading my favorite romances was sweet. It didn't matter that I was reminded about that night every time I walked past the reference section. He'd cheated, and he'd used me to do it. And he'd broken my heart.

But then on a Saturday when the sun was shining and the snow lay thick on the ground, he didn't show up. And suddenly I didn't know how to feel.

CHAPTER FOUR

I'd walked around the library all morning with that anticipation I now felt at the start of every shift. Anticipation at seeing him, followed quickly by shame at the thought, masked quickly after that by anger. *Anger kept me strong.* Anger ensured that no matter how many times he appeared in the library, day after day, I wouldn't give in.

Truth be told, I missed him. For one beautiful snow filled night we'd been together—our bodies and minds joined, soul mates only just discovered. He'd looked deep inside me and seen the walls, then worked out how to climb over them.

I knew I could never get that back. But I missed it all the same.

And then he didn't show up. And instead of anger, instead of shame, instead of anticipation, I felt new emotions. *Disappointment. Fear.*

Maybe he'd had enough. Maybe he'd got the message. And maybe it was the wrong one.

I paced back and forth, distress building for no sensible reason, until Sandra approached to fold me into a warm embrace. "It will be okay, Clara. I'm sure he'll be back next week."

"I don't want him back."

She pulled away from me, eyebrow raised.

"Shut up!" I snapped. "You talk too much."

She laughed. "We've got some new books for the reference section. Why don't you go place them, it will take your mind off things."

* * *

The updated edition of *Essentials of human anatomy and physiology* slid between its companions with a smooth swish. I stood back to admire my handy-work. Sandra had been right. I did feel better—there was something about an ordered row of books that just made you feel…

I paused. Something wasn't right—as the kids might say, my *spider sense* was tingling.

I scanned the shelf. What had caught my eye? Now that I was looking for it, it was hard to see… wait, there it was. One of the books was out of order. I tsked. *Now who would do that?*

A scrap of paper fell to the floor as I pulled out the thick, green tome. I bent to pick up the paper. It contained a single word.

Anarchy…

I recognized the writing. *Booker.* My thumb caressed the cover, tracing the embossed ridges where text was imprinted upon the card. I recognized the book, too.

A smile came to my face, unbidden. He knew me so well. How was that possible, after just one night?

It hadn't been just one night though. I'd seen him every day for the last week. And though I hadn't said a word, he'd been learning about me. What kind of man did that? Put in that amount of effort?

Someone worth breaking the rules for. The answer was there before I could stop it. I tried to push the thought away, but my eyes kept coming back to the book.

There were memories here. Memories that even now I couldn't entirely shut down; that even angry as I was, I couldn't forget. I'd been so happy. Like a princess in a fairytale—an erotic one to be sure; 1001 Arabian nights, perhaps, but a princess in his arms none the less.

I'd never felt that way before. So... treasured.

I opened the book carefully, wary of the memories within. Indian imagery was an erotic art form wholly its own—all long fingers, body jewelry and rounded breasts. But it was the words I was interested in, now. I flicked to the page we had read together—that we had acted out. But when I opened it, I stared in shock.

He'd written on it! He'd written notes in that casual scrawl of his right there in the margins of the page. How... how could he! *This was a library book!*

Scandalized, I began to read. They were notations about how I'd made him feel.

Step 1 had an arrow, with the words *Holy Crap!* penciled beside it.

Step 7: Sucking a Mango Fruit was double underlined with exclamation marks.

Beside *Step 8*, the handwriting was shaky. *As if he'd actually been reliving the memory even as he wrote it.*

And then, at the very bottom of the page, a note written in clear, calm script.

> *How many times I've dreamed of this. The feel of your mouth on my shaft, the smooth slide of your head as it bobs up and down below me.*
>
> *...and yet I'd give it all up for one more kiss. To raise you and have you in my arms beside me.*

I snapped the book shut, the clap echoing in the too silent library. I couldn't—I'd made a promise, all those years ago. I'd broken the rules by accident. I wouldn't break them on purpose. Not again.

CHAPTER FIVE

I didn't want to admit it, but seeing Booker this week had awoken... emotions. Things I had thought buried. Things I hadn't realized I'd felt until he never showed up.

I checked the temperature of the bath and then lit the candles. It was time to forget about all that though. Most people went out on Saturday night. I had another tradition.

I slipped into the water with a sigh, enjoying the just-too-hot heat as it slid up my legs and then my thighs. Wine, a good book, a hot bath. What more could a woman want?

The bath bomb I'd used today had contained rose petals. They floated to the top of the water—tiny, red ballerinas dancing upon its surface. I sunk back and closed my eyes, breathing in the sweet, fragrant scent.

It was on my third glass of wine that I pulled it from its hiding place. I couldn't help it. I'd tried to read something else; one of my favorite stories, a saucy tale that usually got me excited and then very relaxed indeed. But tonight it wasn't working. I kept thinking about... him.

I hadn't smuggled it home, not exactly. I mean, a librarian couldn't technically steal from her own library, could she? I was going to put it back—I'd just wanted to read the comments one more time, that's all.

I ran my finger along the green spine, feeling the embossed lettering. I opened it slowly, careful to dry my fingers first.

I would do this to you, if I could. The words were penciled neatly in the margins of a page showing two lovers intertwined. The page adjacent labelled it *The Lotus Position*.

I began to read the printed text—there were no hand written notes on this page.

> *The man sits cross legged and the woman sits on his lap, facing him, and lowers herself onto his member. The Ananga Ranga suggests that the man place his hands on his partner's shoulders, but I would rather put my arms around your body, or perhaps your neck.*

I flicked to another page, but then flicked back. That hadn't sounded right. I continued to read.

> *Imagine us together, my mouth pressing into yours. My tongue reaching past your lips as, down below, other parts of our bodies mirror our actions.*

I'd read the book, and this was… different. The Kamasutra wasn't meant to speak directly to the reader. It was clinical, a list of instructions. This had been changed somehow. How was that possible? I turned the page.

> *The female stands with back arched against the wall as the male mounts her. Clara lifts a leg to ease his access. Both sigh in delight.*

I sat up, almost spilling my wine. *That was my name!* I opened another page at random. A new position.

Riding the stallion: She mounts Booker in an athletic-

Son of a biscuit! There we were, our names mentioned over and over again. I flicked through the book. Not scrawled in pen—although there were some of these as well—but instead, miraculously, within the very text itself; a part of the book, right there in front of me.

I snapped the book shut with a clap for the second time today. But this time I opened it again after only a slight pause. An idea had occurred to me. An idea so audacious, so ridiculous it couldn't possibly…

The title page confirmed my suspicions. A hand written inscription:

To Clara. A first edition romance we can both enjoy. B

Blow me down and call me shorty, he'd made me a book. A gosh darned, honest to goodness book!

My first thought was that this must have cost a fortune. Like, *literally a fortune*, to turn something like this around in the time that he had.

My second thought was to wonder what else the story contained. I flicked to a random page.

> *Erogenous zones:*
> *It is said that the most potent sexual organ is the brain. You taught me that, Clara. You turned me on with laughter, and wit, and intellect, and imagination. Never have I ever wanted to read a book so badly. Never have I ever wanted a woman so desperately.*

I turned the page.

> *The nipples and surrounding areas are highly sensitive to touch. Some women can reach orgasm by oral stimulation of the nipples alone. I wonder if I could do that for you,*

Clara? If my mouth and tongue, applied with calm precision and excited lapping, could do the same as I did lower, that night of the storm?

The night of the storm… I did remember that. I remembered the feel of being in his arms. The pleasure he created all over my body. Even now, the thought brought shivers to me. Shivers of desire. Shivers of anticipation.

The neck and inside of the arm, too, provide sensations that arouse. The feet, when stimulated, transmit feeling via their nerve endings to all over the body. I would do that to you. I would bath you and massage you, then begin my kisses at your toes and travel slowly upward, lips pressing against your skin, till I gently tickled the underside of your knee. I'd travel further up, but I wouldn't stop at your waist. No. I'd keep going, kissing up the side of your body until I reached your neck, where I'd linger.

I couldn't help it—my free hand went to my neck, feeling his kisses as brushes upon my skin, imagining him before me.

I'd nibble you gently, careful not to leave a mark—that will come later—then begin my downward journey once more. But this time, my mouth would find your breasts. My tongue would circle gently.

My hand slid from my neck slowly as I read, until it was gently tracing a nipple. I was getting shivers—my body turned on from the words before me.

With my hands I'd knead your other breast, enjoying its fullness, the feel of it between my fingers. I like your breasts; I dream about them. I'd pinch each nipple sharply, then cover them again with my mouth; sucking the brief, pleasurable pain way.

I squeezed my nipple between thumb and forefinger, mirroring his words. I wanted him so badly. I wanted him here, right now, to do the things he was describing.

> *Then my hand would move lower, my mouth remaining where it was; your senses splitting to reveal electricity slowly building within your bosom as the skin over your thighs began to goose bump in anticipation of the hand moving slowly toward it.*

My hand slipped between my thighs with a whisper. I knew what was coming. And I knew I had to keep reading until I got there. The beating of my heart, the quickness of my breath; neither would let me turn away now.

> *Only now that my hand has reached your most tender of places does my head, too, slide down. My hand pauses in its caress, to part your legs, allowing room between them. Your center is open to me, a beautiful rose, with a fragrance that I need to inhale. My lips kiss it lovingly—soft kisses that lap against its edges. Above, I can hear you begin to moan.*

A hiss of air escaped my lips as my legs widened in the bath. The water eddied gently against them, creating delicious ripples that tantalized as they washed upon me.

My fingers began to circle. If I closed my eyes I could imagine him there, between my legs. The water swirled like his tongue, smelling of roses and feeling like heaven. The pressure from his mouth would get firmer as he listened to my breathing, as he noted the tension in my thighs. He'd know the effect he was having on me. My fingers began to circle faster as my eyes opened.

> *I take your bud within my mouth and begin to suck gently, teasing it out, letting it slide between my lips before taking it within once more. I love the feel of it in my mouth, this*

opportunity to show you the pleasure you have already shown me. My hands find your opening and one finger inches gently inside—just the tip, running around the edge. I can tell you want more. You're so wet. And so suddenly I do what your eyes have been begging for. I thrust inside, my finger entering you all the way.

I moaned as my own hand followed suit. The heat of the bath was nothing to the warmth growing between my legs, the excitement building within my thighs. I began to tremble with each slide of my finger in and out.

You want me to finish you, I know it. But we're not done yet. We've only just begun. You beg me, but in answer I slide a second finger within. They curl slightly toward the top, placing pressure within you as my arm begins to move.

I could feel him within me. Pleasuring me. The water in the tub began to slosh against the sides. My toes began to curl.

The movements get faster. Faster. We're on the home stretch now, I can't stop myself. You can't, either.

My back began to arch. This was it. The heat was a bonfire raging inside me.

Your body is on fire with the pleasure I'm producing within you. You start to buck upon my fingers. You start to screa-

I threw the book to the floor as I screamed in pleasure, every muscle in my hips suddenly contracting in desire. Flames of delight were ripping through my body, clouding my mind to everything except the delight this one man had wrought upon me.

It felt like forever until I slumped back against the bath; breathless, replete and satisfied like I hadn't been in weeks. I lay there until my breathing returned to normal.

Then I reached to the floor and picked up the book once more, turning to the very last page. I was weary yes— that blissful, floating laziness which only happened after the best of times was slowly creeping upon me—but I wanted to read the end. I had to see how the book finished.

I smiled. The last page had just three words, printed in neat text in the center of the white page. Then I closed the book and placed it, more carefully this time, onto the floor. Three little words.

To be continued...

CHAPTER SIX

In the light of day, the hopes and dreams of last night began to fade. So what if he had written a book just for me? So what if he knew me so well that he could make me orgasm not just once, but again and again as I lay in bed later that night?

A knock sounded at the front door. Who could be calling this early on a Sunday morning? I leapt toward it eagerly, earlier thoughts forgotten. "Book-"

"Oh." A tall gentleman dressed in trench coat and ratty face stood before me. "Um, hi. Who are you?"

"I might ask the same question of you, Miss…?"

I frowned. "That's none of your business. Whatever you're selling, I don't want it."

A foot wedged between the door as I closed it. "But I think you do, Clara."

I paused. "How do you know my name?"

His body pushed against the door, and then he was inside. "I know a lot about you—librarian, divorced, no kids. But what I don't know—what I want to know, is what happened several weeks ago when you were stuck in the library overnight with one Booker DeVale."

"DeVale? Is that his last name?"

"I work for *Mrs. Stacey DeVale*, the gentleman in question's wife. You may or may not be aware that Mr. DeVale is a very wealthy man; they are going through a very messy divorce right now."

A hand went to his pocket. He pulled out a cigarette, but didn't light it. "I have been charged by Mrs. DeVale to investigate the truth behind rumors that her husband may or may not have been unfaithful to her during the course of their contract."

The first thought to enter my mind was a question. "Have... there been other women, then?" *I didn't know if I wanted to know the answer.*

The private investigator's mouth screwed up like he'd ingested something distasteful. The cigarette went back in his pocket. "No. Not as of yet, more's the shame. That's why I'm here."

"Wait, what do you mean, 'more's the shame?'"

"My apologies, a slip of the tongue. My client saw you two together in the snow when she picked him up. She is hoping you may be amendable to giving her some information on the matter."

My hand was starting to tremble. I held it firmly with my other, before he could see. "Is she angry?"

He shook his head. "On the contrary, she would be delighted. Very little love is lost between the two right now. She'd be willing to pay you very handsomely for any information you might be willing to give her."

I hated Booker. Or at least, that's what I told myself. But I wasn't going to poison that one night between us with something like this. "I'm sorry Mr... what did you say your name was?"

"Simon Wickson, Private Investigator,"

"Well I'm sorry Mr. Wickson. I can't help you."

He looked at me, eyebrow arched. "Really. Even though he's been back to your library every day since? Even though you opened the door saying his name?"

"I believe he's overseeing the renovations next door," I said, quoting words said to me by Booker himself. "And last time I checked it was a free library. Are you going to tell me he's not allowed inside?"

"Not at all." He placed a calling card in my hand. "But please, if you do see him again, or you remember anything else, give me a call. I can make it very worth your while— and I promise after, you'll never see him again."

"I cannot bound a pitch above dull woe," I whispered. "Under love's heavy burden do I sink."

"What was that?"

"It's from Romeo and Juliet," I said, closing the door behind him. "You wouldn't understand."

CHAPTER SEVEN

I awoke that night to the beautiful strains of instrumental music. I lay in bed, confused. Noise was common in the street below my second floor apartment, but it was always fast and angry—the reverberations of an engine, or the blaring of a stereo. This soft music, in comparison, was as if spring had been distilled and then left to air beneath my very window.

I wrapped myself in a dressing gown and shuffled to the balcony, the music growing louder as the door slid open.

My mouth opened in shock. A string quartet was arranged on the lawn below, their suits dark against the white snow in the starlight. Standing behind them, dressed in the most immaculate tuxedo with hands clasped behind his back, was-

"Booker? Is that you?"

He looked up, a smile lighting his face. From behind his back he drew a single, long stemmed rose. "Clara!"

"What the heck are you doing? It's one o'clock in the morning!"

He performed an elegant bow, and then indicated the rose. "Serenading you, of course."

"You're what?"

"Serenading you. If there's one thing I've learned from reading romances, it's that the heroine always falls for a gentleman if he serenades her by moonlight."

"Are you out of you mind?"

"I tell you as much, because I do not wish you to think that my illness is feigned. But supposing the illness had been a mere trick to frighten you, what a risk the rascal would have run!"

I paused briefly to process that last sentence. "Are you quoting *Casanova* now?"

"As the good man himself said, 'Love is a great poet, its resources are inexhaustible, but if the end it has in view is not obtained, it feels weary and remains silent.'"

Lights were beginning to come on up and down the street. The old lady across the road was already on her front step, hand on her heart.

"Booker," I said flatly. "Go home."

"No. Not until you let me explain."

"There's nothing to explain. You're married."

"I will begin with this confession: whatever I have done in the course of my life, whether it be good or evil, has been done freely; I am a free agent."

"Booker," I said, exasperated. "Stop quoting Casanova."

"Because a few thorns are to be found in a basket full of roses, is the existence of those beautiful flowers to be denied? No; it is a slander to deny that life is happiness."

Across the road, the old lady gave him a thumbs up.

"Booker!"

"I will not stop until you let me up."

I crossed my arms. "No."

"Would the great lover himself have taken that answer?"

I glared at him.

"Then I won't either," he said, ignoring my look. He opened his arms wide. "And I threw myself into her burning arms, passionate with love, and gave her the most ardent proof of this for seven hours straight."

I blushed, knowing exactly at what he was hinting. "It wasn't quite seven hours, sir."

"Five then. What can I say? Time seemed to stand still. I wished it would never end. And yet I dreaded each passing moment, for it brought us closer to the morning. 'We kissed whatever took our fancy, and just as she applied her lips to the mouth of the pistol, it went off and the discharge inundated her face and her bosom. She was delighted, and watched the process to the end with all the curiosity of a doctor.'"

The old lady cackled loudly. "Let him up dearie! Or move aside and let me have a go!"

I turned instantly bright red. "Booker! You're embarrassing me."

"Nonsense. I'm simply telling the world that I love you, and you love me, despite what you protest." He raised his voice, arms in the air as if speaking now to the street. "And if that love happens to include the most amazing sex I've ever had, then so be it." He grinned, a cheeky thing that made his eyes sparkle. "I'll freely admit it, and I'll keep on admitting it, loudly, until you let me apologize, and explain."

I stomped my foot in the cold night air. I really should have wrapped something warmer around myself than this flimsy dressing gown. "That's not fair!"

"Life is not fair." He took a deep breath, about to quote more verse.

"Oh shush!" I said, cutting him off. "Get up here. You've got exactly five minutes."

I swear the old lady was cheering as I opened the front door.

* * *

I couldn't help it. I made him a cup of hot chocolate.

He took an appreciative sip from the steaming hot mug, then winked at me. "Thank you," he said warmly.

"You can thank me when you leave," I said archly. "Right now, I want to know how you found me, what you're really doing standing in the snow, and why the heck you haven't gotten the message yet." I paused, considering my words. "And not, necessarily, in that order."

He put the cup down, lifting a hand to tick points off on his fingers. "Firstly, money can buy almost anything. Second, the one thing money can't buy, is love. And third," he said. "You're giving me the wrong message. It's not what I want to hear. And I know it's not what your heart wants to say."

"You know nothing."

"I know we spent a night together that I didn't want to end. I'm trying to stop it from ending. I'm hoping you feel the same way."

It wasn't a question I was prepared to answer. "Then why didn't you come to the library yesterday?"

His hand went to the back of his neck. "There were, ah, complications I had to attend to."

"What kind of complications?"

The hand rounded his head to brush over his face.

"You're married," I said for him.

He nodded.

"You know how I feel about that."

"I do, now..." he paused. "What I mean," he said, holding his hands before him, "is that most people, myself included, don't like the idea of cheating. I'm not asking for forgiveness for that."

The hand reached to rub the back of his neck once more. "But something, I'm not sure what, happened in your past. I'm sorry I didn't know about that. I'm sorry I didn't know how my actions would be taken."

He took a deep breath. "Clara, my wife and I are together in name only. We haven't been in love for a long time; she already lives with someone else. I thought to explain, but just never found the right time. And then I thought, well, the paperwork would be through shortly. If I didn't tell you, it might not even matter."

"Shortly?" I asked. "But not yet."

He grimaced. "It was supposed to be signed the night I crashed. That's why I was flying in the storm—anything to get this over and done with."

There was something he hadn't told me. *Not yet.* I asked the obvious question first. "Then why hasn't it happened by now?"

His eyes met mine. "You."

"Me? What do I have to do with this?"

He leaned forward. "There was a pre-nup Clara. Something I signed when I was young and stupid and poor."

"And?"

"And it has a clause. One that gives everything to my wife should I ever be unfaithful."

"But… didn't you say she's living with someone already?"

He shook his head. "The clause is very specific." He closed his eyes, reciting. "*Should either party engage in relations of a sexual nature with a person outside of the marriage, that person will forfeit all wealth, including land, stock, and cash reserves, to the other party; on the proviso that concrete evidence can be presented in a court of law incriminating either the cheating partner or their mistress.*"

I shrugged, puzzled. "What's the problem—it seems you both have a case against each other, shouldn't they cancel out?"

"Listen to that last line again," he said. "Either the cheating partner, or their *mistress*."

The issue dawned like moonlight on a murky night. "*Their mistress.* It only counts if you cheat with a woman."

He nodded. "When I couldn't make it that night, we were arranged to sign the following morning. That's why she picked us up. But then she saw you, and she put two and two together… and well, now she's hungry."

For a moment—the briefest of moments, I felt compassion for the man sitting before me. What must it have been like, to live years with someone you don't love? To finally see the end in sight, then have it snatched away?

But then my resolve hardened. I couldn't answer that. But I could answer something else. *What must it be like to be the third party?*

And then suddenly, desperately, I needed to know the answer to one more question. "This money you're fighting over. Is it more important than me?"

He sat back. "Clara. No, of course not."

"Then tell your wife about us." *I'd heard too many promises in my life.*

"Clara, you don't understand."

I rose, trembling. "I think I do." *I'd seen too many promises broken already.* "You're still married, and whether it is only by the letter of the law or not doesn't matter! All I see is another cheating bastard that guarantees the world but shows up empty handed."

"Clara-"

"Get out."

"Clara, please."

"GET OUT!" I screamed. My finger stabbed toward the door. "Get out, get out, get out!"

He stood, face like stone, and walked out the door.

I reached for the business card in my pocket. Then I picked up the phone.

CHAPTER EIGHT

"In vain I have struggled. It will not do. My feelings will not be repressed. You must allow me to tell you how ardently I admire and love you."

"Booker don't, please. This was a mistake."

"You can hardly doubt the purport of my discourse; my attentions have been too marked to be mistaken."

I sighed. Maybe it had been a bad idea to meet at the library. I had forgotten how embarrassing Booker could be. "Do you always quote the books you read?"

"Only when I'm trying to impress someone with the fact that I'm reading *Pride and Prejudice* because it's her favorite book."

It had all seemed so simple—take back control of my life. Teach Booker the consequences of breaking the rules.

But then the private detective had knocked on my door in the middle of the night, looking as fresh as a daisy and as hungry as a shark.

"Thank you for inviting me over. You're doing the right thing. Nobody deserves to be treated the way he's treating you."

"He's actually been kind of sweet. All week he's-"

"Yes, yes. But you're forgetting that you're the victim here. He used you, then tried to cover it up. Did Clinton get away with it? Did Schwarzenegger?"

"Umm."

"Exactly. They each cheated on their partners, and they each had to pay. Might I add that the partners got very handsome rewards for their honesty, too."

I'd told him very firmly that I didn't want money.

"I know. You're doing it because you're angry. He practically raped you!"

"No, that's going too far. He did nothing of the sort."

"It was worth a try—would have made the case stronger. But we'll make it worth your while anyway."

"Maybe… um, maybe this isn't such a good idea after all."

"Nonsense. You can't back out now. You've already admitted to it."

I'd shaken my head, confused. *"Yes. But, I was angry when I called you."*

The Private Investigator had put his hands on my shoulders, leaning in so close I could smell the onion on his breath. *"You don't want to back out of this now. It wouldn't be good for you."*

"Is… is that a threat?" I'd tried to pull away.

His hands had gripped my shoulders, keeping me where I was. *"Of course not. Blackmail is a federal offense which carries serious jail time. I'm merely pointing out that Perjury is a jailable offense too."*

"We're not in court."

"Not yet. But my client is a very powerful, very angry woman. You might want to ask Mr. DeVale about her hunting habits. And what she does to people who get in her way."

He'd smiled at me then, a shark in a salesman's suit. *"Look, there's two ways to do this. One of those ways involves both your names being dragged through the mud. The other involves you getting everything you want. The end result is the same in both cases. Be smart, please."*

The anger had burned too high—unsustainable for more than the time it took to make the call. But I'd still found myself texting Booker with trembling fingers. I'd still found myself wearing a wire in my cleavage; the microphone recording to a USB on my back.

I could feel it there now, as I stood before him. "Booker, you need to go. Your wife-"

"A lady's imagination is very rapid; it jumps from admiration to love, from love to matrimony, in a moment."

"Booker, I'm serious!" I thought back to the private detective. To his greasy, gropey hands as they strapped on my wire. "I... can't do this."

He moved closer. So close that I could smell his cologne. So close I could kiss him, if I but tilted my head. "But I think you can. 'You have taught me to hope,'" he quoted, "'as I have scarcely ever allowed myself to hope before. I know enough of your disposition to be certain that, had you been absolutely, irrevocably decided against me, you would have acknowledged it frankly and openly.'"

The reply sprung unbidden to my lips. The heroine's reply, from the book. "Yes, you know enough of my frankness to believe me capable of that." I trembled as I spoke the next sentence. "After abusing you so abominably to your face, I could have no scruple in abusing you to all your relations."

His hand rose to cup my face, to tilt it toward him. "What we did was so beautiful I dream about it nightly. Tell the whole world and I wouldn't care."

"Do you mean that? Really mean it?"

"Yes. Love knows no rules, Clara. I know you've felt it too."

"But I always follow the rules," I whispered. "And you're married." Always, it came down to this. The stumbling block I could never, ever, get over.

"By the letter of the law, I am. Yes. But not by its heart." He took my hand and placed it against his chest. I could feel it beating within. "Everything I've ever done, ever since I've met you, has been for you. There is nothing more important—not money, not land, not life itself."

He took a deep breath. "I know this is my last chance Clara. You're my angel. A Goddess gracing the earth. And I want you to know that if you walk away, I won't be angry. If you truly can't break free of the rules you've chained yourself in—rules that are right in technicality only—then I know I'll only hurt you more by forcing you against them. I want you to be happy. More than anything."

His hand went to the back of his neck then, and he laughed. "God, look at me—the romantic fool. You've done this to me. This and your blasted books—*Pride and Prejudice* has a lot to answer for."

In the book, the blame was equally shared. Elizabeth who had the pride, and Mister Darcy who had the prejudice. It occurred to me that here, I was the one with both. I looked at him, and in that instant I knew so much.

I knew I loved him. More than anything. More, even, than the rules themselves.

And I knew I'd ruined it. My only chance at happiness, and the wire burning between my breasts had swallowed every word, churning his declaration of love through the sausage grinder of deceit, spitting it out on the other side as something I knew he'd never be able to swallow.

My hands began to tremble. He was the one. The one I could break the rules for. *And I didn't deserve him.* I had to tell him. He deserved, at least, to hear my betrayal in person. "Booker... I-"

"Clara. I know."

"No you don't!" I exclaimed, suddenly angry. "That's the whole point! I'm not who you think I am—I'm not an angel. I'm not a Goddess."

"You are."

"Three years ago Booker. Three years ago I cheated on another man I loved. Who's to say that won't happen again?"

"I'm to say. I won't let you get bored with me. I won't give you a reason to cheat."

I burst into tears. "You're wrong. I already have."

"Really?" He raised an eyebrow, his hand stretching toward me. Then he reached down, and plucked the microphone from between my breasts.

"Are we talking about this?"

CHAPTER NINE

"Booker, I'm so sorry. What I've done is unforgivable. I need to go."

I tried to walk away but he caught my arm, pulling me back. "Wait. You don't understand."

"I do." I said, turning to him. "And I'm sorry Booker. You've been so good to me. You're perfect. Perfect in every way. And I've… I've *fudged* it up big time." Tears began to well. Three years I'd waited for happiness. And then, when it was presented on a silver platter, I'd dashed it to the ground for money and spite. "I don't deserve you. But, the recordings, I want you to know I'm not going to give them to her."

Booker's hand went to the back of his neck. And then he pulled out his phone. "I need to call my wife."

I leapt to his arm before he could dial. "Wait! I said she doesn't have them!"

Against everything I expected, he pulled me to him, kissing me savagely. I stumbled backward in shock, then looked around quickly. We were in the library, after all.

"I'm not angry at you," he said. "I'm angry at myself. I've let this go on for far too long."

He dialed a number quickly, and I heard a female voice answer. "Stacey? I don't want to do this anymore," he said. "You win. I'll sign the documents tomorrow."

More noise from the other end of the phone.

"Yes. Everything. It's all yours. It's worth nothing without love. I hope you realize that one day." The call ended with a click.

He put it away as I stared at him with open mouth. "What did you just do?" I whispered.

"What I should have done a long time ago. Stopped hiding."

"But… your money!"

His hand went to my chin, stroking it, and suddenly it was as if the storm clouds lifted. He smiled. "My dear, you're the one that taught me the value of that."

"What do you mean?"

"What I was trying to do wasn't working. What is life, if you're not living? What is money if you're not happy? I don't care about any of that. I care about you. And I don't want you to walk away. Not ever again."

I looked up at him. Into his strong face, his piercing eyes. "Can we really make this work?"

In answer, he leaned down and kissed me.

We parted with a whisper of breath that trailed across my upper lip, giving me shivers. I had goosebumps all over my body. And suddenly the past didn't matter. For either of us.

I didn't care about what had happened three years ago. He didn't care about what had happened three seconds ago. The emotion in his eyes mirrored mine—*all that mattered was one more kiss.*

I took his hand, leading him deeper into the stacks. And then we were kissing again, deeply, like we'd never kissed before; the passion of new lovers, the confidence of old. I knew this man, though I'd only known him one night. I could read his desire for me in the way his hands roamed my body, in the quickness of his breath, in the urgency of his mouth on mine.

His hand reached for my waist, running up the side of my dress until it reached my breasts, caressing them, cupping them roughly through the smooth material. His other hand slipped down to my legs, sliding up, pulling the skirt with it.

I wiggled from his grasp. "Not here."

"I want you. Right now."

I shook my head. I couldn't. Not with other people so close.

"Come with me," he said urgently. He pulled me swiftly toward the front door, and then as Sandra looked on in shock, lifted me giggling into his arms to carry me out the internal doors and down the hallway. We stopped beside the still unfinished café. A quick jingle of keys, and then we were tumbling through it, kissing once more.

We were in a world of books and forest; green vines and potted trees, recycled timber and recycled books. Tables lay between ferns. Books lined the walls everywhere plants didn't.

"Booker, this is beautiful!"

He pulled me to him, swinging the door closed with a leg, then pushed us both back until I was against a table. His hand went behind me, fiddling, and then my dress slid downward. It pooled against the cool countertop. "You're beautiful."

The fabric slid like silk down my legs as I wiggled myself briefly off the table. I flicked it off, one foot at a time.

My bra was next, short work for his deft fingers, the lace catching on by breasts until, shyly, I pulled it from my body, one arm protecting my modesty.

Gently, he peeled it away. "I want to see you, my goddess. All of you." My breasts sprung free.

With their release fell the microphone. It dropped to the floor. And suddenly I no longer felt erotic. I felt dirty. *Could he really forgive me? Could I ever forgive myself?* I wanted to kick it, stomp it in furious anger.

I raised my foot but Booker stooped to catch my calf. He bent to one knee. "No Clara. Now is not the time for anger. If this is what it took for us to be together, then so be it." He pulled my shoes off, kissing each foot gently as he did. "I've made my choice. And I choose you." Then he began to kiss slowly upward, lips pressing softly against my skin, tickling the underside of my knee, traveling ever further up. He kissed my hips, then my waist. Then my breasts. And then he was at my neck.

My head tilted backward, opening myself to him. I'd tried being angry. I'd tried being guilty. Now it was time to finally be free.

I felt his kiss on my collarbone. Then hot breath as his lips moved to my neck. He bit me, gently, just once. The move felt inexplicably familiar. Goosebumps broke out down my side.

His hands moved to my breasts, kneading them. I could feel them pressed between his fingers, the gentle caresses alternating with rough pressing. It felt… good. It felt like I was his to do with as he wanted, as my body could make him mine.

He pinched a nipple, a sharp sensation that sent a thrill of exquisite pain through me; then covered it quickly with his mouth, sucking the brief, pleasurable ache way. Again it felt familiar, the memory of a beautiful pleasure I was to experience once again. My loins began to ache. I wanted him so badly.

One hand moved lower, his mouth continuing to suckle my breasts, and my senses split; electricity building within my bosom, the skin over my thighs goose bumping in anticipation of the hand moving slowly toward it. It reached the space between my legs. And suddenly I knew why this felt so familiar. Why it was so exquisitely exciting.

I'd read it before.

I gasped as his hand began to circle. "The book!"

His lips left my breast to rise and kiss me on the mouth. "I was wondering if you'd read it," he said with a grin. "You know what comes next then, don't you?"

I nodded, breathless, as he slid slowly to his knees.

"And does that please you?" His lips grazed my flesh, sending shivers shooting through my body.

I reached down to grasp his hair, then pressed him in to me. *Yes. It pleased me immensely.*

I gave a small moan as he set to work; mouth nuzzling into me, sending shivers through my body with each tiny flicker of his tongue. I widened my legs and the small flickers became longer rasps as he sensed my enthusiasm deepening.

And then I felt his hands on my thighs, slipping up my smooth skin. I looked down in time to see his head lift off, a finger sliding into his mouth, wetting it. The head returned; the finger followed. I felt it at my edges as his lips kissed my pearl above, each circle a hint at the indescribable pleasure to come, each kiss a burst of electricity through my body. And then, in one smooth motion, his finger entered me all the way. "Son of a Biscuit!" I groaned. My hands moved to grip the table behind me, legs in danger of buckling. "That feels so good!"

He began to pump faster; his arm working in time with his mouth, building the most delicious feeling in my legs that I thought must soon escape and flood my body. It was like the friction had produced a tiny spark that was now arcing back and forth between my hips, growing stronger with each second, with each movement of his hand and tongue.

I pulled him up. "I want you. Now."

His hand remained inside when he stood. "Time enough for that later. We're following a storyline here, remember?" The other hand slipped to the hair at the base of my neck. His lips locked with mine. Then he tugged, sharply.

I groaned into his mouth. "That wasn't in the book," I panted.

"Sometimes, stories change," he growled. Then he kissed me savagely, and it took my breath away with its ferocity.

His hand began to move again with forceful, powerful motions. Motions that said he wouldn't be denied. That I should hold on for the ride.

And the small arcs of pleasure suddenly doubled in size, becoming balls of electricity that zinged around my body. It felt like my hair must be standing on end—my toes were certainly curling.

He moved faster, and then faster again; my breathing following suit until I was gasping, eyes wide with each thrust of his fingers and each sharp tug as he kissed my lips and exposed neck.

"I'm close. So close," I moaned.

His hand left my neck to find my pearl once more. He kissed me again, and then pinched it sharply. The effect was electric. I'd never experienced this… this pleasure and pain, all wrapped up so tightly that I didn't know which was which. *I liked it.*

He was pressing me into the table behind us now, or perhaps I was collapsed against it. The only thing I was aware of was him at my hips—the movement inside me. My emotions were awhirl. I couldn't think straight. Time was bending.

And then all of a sudden he dropped to his knees, and his face was pressing into me once more, and he was kissing me with his fingers still inside; the most delicate of licks to counter the rapid motions just below.

I couldn't help it; the spark had become a lightning bolt. I threw back my head and screamed my pleasure as electricity arced through my nerves, sending my vision white, making my body helpless. I could do nothing but hold on, the lightning a wild, untamed thing controlled entirely by the man below.

His fingers held me upright until my body finally stopped shuddering. And then he withdrew, and my legs couldn't support me anymore. I slid to the floor, struggling to breathe.

"Bow my legs and call me Bambi," I struggled out when I could talk. "If this is what it's going to be like when we're together, I need to start going to the gym."

"Did you like how that story ended?"

I climbed shakily to my feet, nodding.

"Yes. Very much. Although you got one thing very wrong."

He looked at me quizzically. "And what's that?"

I pushed him up against a wall. "The story's not over. It's just beginning."

I began tearing at his clothes madly, his own hands joining in until shortly we were both panting, standing as naked as Adam and Eve in the garden of Eden.

His body was just as I'd remembered it. Just as I'd dreamed every night since. *Hard and lithe. Powerful arms that were thick and strong. Hairless chest heavy with muscle; abs that flexed and rippled with each hot, heavy pant of his mouth.*

His hands went to my hips, pulling me close, hard against his erect member. I could feel it pressing against my stomach. I could sense its urgency.

He turned me then, flipped me around, to bend me over. I felt pressure, briefly, as he positioned himself.

Then he entered me.

I gasped. I could feel his smooth length as it slipped inside my wet center. I could feel it as it slid all the way in, filling me, possessing me.

I leaned back into him and he groaned. One of his hands went to my hip. The other stretched to my shoulder. And then he was driving me, hard and fast, our thighs meeting in rapid slaps.

"I'm not going to last long Clara. I've been wanting this for too long. I want it too bad."

"Good." I needed to feel him in me—all of him. I needed to know I could make him lose control. "Do it for me. Now."

Our motions got faster, more frantic. I could sense him building with every breath, with every tightening of his fingers.

It was so hot, this power I had over his body. So hot the way he looked at me, the things I could make him do. I began to build too—faster than I'd thought possible, the pleasure pounding into my body with each thrust of his hard member. His hands moved to my hips. I braced myself against a table. And then he was slamming into me over and over with such force that my hair was flying with each slap and my body had that electricity back; that delicious storm that must break at any moment over us both.

I began to cry out his name. He cried out mine. And then I felt him release inside me, and it tipped me over the edge, too. Our bodies stilled, while inside us, the entire universe writhed in ecstasy, convulsing over and over with each sharp pump of his long, hard member.

We had barely paused before he turned me to him, picking me up to lay me over one of the tables.

"Again?" I asked, panting.

"Are you complaining?" He stood before me, then slipped himself inside, slowly this time, and I moaned a reply that spelled my answer with indistinct syllables.

This was different to the last time. But just as good. I could feel every inch of him as he slid in and out; the motions slow enough now to be distinct. Slow enough to produce a different kind of electricity—a warm, fuzzy static as opposed to a fast, hard zing.

"Let's do this every day Clara. Over and over for the rest of our lives."

"You've got to get divorced first." The words didn't hurt like they used to—didn't fill me with horror. Now they excited me; gave me something to look forward to. He was mine. *And he was worth the wait.*

I sat up, propping myself against the table with one hand to kiss him, legs wrapped around his waist. I could see his muscles flexing as his hips moved back and forth into me. I could feel the result inside.

He picked me up, and suddenly my entire weight was suspended on him, and I was being lifted up and down on the railroad of his shaft, traveling its length, his biceps flexing with each motion. I began to moan louder, thrilled by the strength of his arms; by what he could do to me.

He kissed me, cutting off the moans, and then we were groaning into each other's mouths until he lay me down once more on the table, but this time lifting my legs high, resting them on his shoulders. His motions began to quicken.

Short little flares of pleasure were bursting through me. The angle was just right. I moaned for him to go faster, my hands reaching up to his chest, and he obliged.

I could feel his heartbeat as he began to work me. I could smell our sweat. I began to move with him, grinding into him, moving him faster and faster as those flares of pleasure grew, becoming spinning balls of light within my hips and my throat and my heart.

Soon we were at full speed once more, and I was close—those flares were threatening to take over my body, to explode inside of me. He was close too—I could tell it in his breathing, in the groans that were issuing from his body. I struggled to hold on, to wait for him, but he felt so good.

My hands moved from his chest down his hard stomach to that part where the both of us met. I could feel his hair there, feel each wet and slippery slide into my being. I let my fingers linger over him; feeling him as he slid in and out, moistening them on the rhythmically exposed lengths of his hard member. Then I moved them to myself. *Oh gosh. There.*

I couldn't help it. I began to circle my pearl, faster and faster, the spinning balls of light now out of control inside me, growing exponentially larger until they were filling my being. His own thrusts became urgent. My fingers circled-

The light exploded inside of me, filling my mind as my whole body contracted in ecstasy; my hips tensing, to grip him helplessly.

I felt him swell against the sudden increase of pressure. "Clara!"

He threw back his head, and then the balls of light were within him too, and I could feel his love inside me, taking me to even greater heights. I screamed in pleasure, unable to keep this feeling inside, as we writhed on the table together; each one setting off the other in a chain reaction that just kept going and going and going until we were both collapsed, spent, upon the table.

"Call me Bambi indeed…" I panted, when I was finally able to talk.

He leaned up on one elbow before me. "And we made love like two hummingbirds, fast and furious, and then again like wild beasts, and I never wanted it to end; this primal mating of mine."

"Casanova?" I asked, uncertain.

He shook his head. "Booker. Which is much better."

PART 3:

BY THE SEA

The idea is simple. An extravagant holiday to spend as much money as Booker and Clara can before it all gets taken away.

But Booker isn't telling Clara the whole truth. There's another reason they're going to his private tropical island. A reason that could see Booker dead, and Clara in jail.

What could be important enough for him to risk everything? And who is the mysterious woman Clara spies kissing Booker when they arrive?

The story continues in *By the Sea*.

PROLOGUE

I walked into the kitchen to find Booker already up, a steaming mug of coffee held in both hands. He was staring out at the balcony, deep in thought.

My arms went around his neck "Big day today, hey Mr. Lover?"

It had been two weeks since the events in the library. Two weeks since Booker had rung his wife to tell her he was getting a divorce, and she was getting everything else. I still couldn't believe it—the man was giving up everything: his entire, vast fortune for me.

I'd been wearing a wire… and then he'd found out, and… well, I'd never given the recordings over, but he'd said he'd sign the documents anyway.

It had taken all this time to work out the details; a team of lawyers working day and night—my first clue to exactly how wealthy Booker actually was. He'd never said, and I'd never asked—it seemed poor form when the man was about to give it all up; but it must be millions—and all for me. Snatches of conversation about boats, companies and cars hinted it could be even more.

Booker turned to me, kissing my arm. "You're up."

"I am."

I hesitated. "Booker, you don't have to do this." *Today was the day he was meant to sign.*

He kissed me again. "You don't know my wife. Now that she's found that loophole, she's hungry. Even if I did say no, her agents would just hound us until she got something—a kiss snapped on a telephoto lens, a conversation on a bugged phone. I don't want our life to be like that."

"Isn't there something we could do?" I'd asked it a hundred times, but still, each time I hoped for a different answer.

He shook his head. "The only solution would be to never see you again. And that's not acceptable. Because she won't give up, and I won't give up you."

He pulled me into his lap. "But I do have an… idea."

I raised an eyebrow. "Why am I suspicious all of a sudden?"

"Because you know me so well, that's why."

I sighed. "Alright. Out with it. What's this idea?"

"So it's like this. The minute I sign those documents, I lose everything."

"I never wanted your money, Booker."

"I know. It's one of the reasons I'm here right now." He took a deep breath. "Bu-ut…"

"Yes?"

He grinned at me. "Wouldn't you like to spend it?"

CHAPTER ONE

"This… is not what I expected."

Booker had suggested a vacation, and half an hour later, we had walked out the door.

Well Booker had walked. I'd been carried, his spontaneity so terrifying that when he got sick of my excuses he'd picked me up and forcibly transported me, squealing, to the limousine.

It was terrifying. But also liberating; Sandra was going to cover my shifts at work, I'd paid my rent in advance, and there was literally nothing else keeping us here.

And so we'd stepped into a private jet in freezing cold snow, and stepped out of it into tropical sunshine; our flight shortened considerably by Moet and some very athletic sex, to a country where I couldn't understand a word the locals said, but the food was delicious. And I was hungry, let me tell you—most likely from all that exercise on the plane.

Our first stop, once we got in the limousine, was to get food. Booker seemed to know what he was doing on this account, directing the driver along crowded side roads before stopping at a street cart on an otherwise innocuous corner. "I know it's not a five star restaurant," he said, motioning for a handful of chicken skewers out the rolled down window, then paying with a hundred dollar bill. He told the stall holder to keep the change. "But trust me, this is better."

I looked at him dubiously, but eventually shrugged my shoulders. *Relationships were all about trust, right?* I took a bite.

"Color me flabbergasted—this is delicious!" I exclaimed. "How on earth did you know about this?"

He grinned. "I've been here a lot—it's the launching point for our holiday."

"You mean this isn't the end spot?" Booker hadn't told me where we were going; only that it involved a short cruise. "Because we could just put up a tent beside that chicken stall and I'd be happy!" The funny thing was, I was half serious—the chicken was amazing.

We arrived a short while later at the town's port, a bustling hive of small boats. One corner was dominated by a towering white cruiser larger than all the others combined; a superyacht 200 feet long if it was an inch.

We began to head toward it.

"No. Surely not… is that yours?" I asked incredulously.

Booker broke into a grin. "It's a beauty, isn't it?"

"It's the biggest boat I've ever seen! There are cruise ships that are smaller!"

He chuckled. "It's one of my bigger ones, for certain. But I think you'll find it nice."

"You have more than one? Exactly how wealthy are you?" I asked, eyes narrowed. Each time I thought I'd figured Booker out, he threw another curve ball at me.

He shook his head, face momentarily clouding. "It doesn't matter. Stacey will own it all, soon." Then the smile was back, and he clapped his hands. "Come on—this baby costs upward of 10 Grand a day when it's in use. Let's see how much of her money we can spend before we have to give it up."

* * *

"So what do you think?" Booker asked once we'd done the tour. We'd already left the harbor, cruising out into the blue open ocean, leaving the rest of the world behind.

What did I think? My jaw had been open for so long that my mouth was dry. The *Leaf* was three levels of decadence the likes of which I'd never seen before. It had a lap pool, sundeck, cocktail bar and a master bedroom bigger than my apartment, with a wardrobe full of designer clothes, all in my size (I had Booker's assistant to thank for that one). It had a speedboat mounted in the hull, and twin Jet Skis too, both capable of being launched through doors at water level at the back of the boat. It had French crystal wine glasses and an entire cellar full of liquid to put in them; both looked older than I was.

The top deck was a completely private paradise, off limits to the crew, with a huge 20 person Jacuzzi and the most amazing view over the ocean. In case you got sick of the view, a retractable cinema screen could rise at the press of a button. I assumed it was so you could sip champagne as the sun set and watch yourself on *Lifestyles of the Rich and Famous*.

But none of these were the best part. *Oh no.* The best part was where we were standing right now. "I thought you didn't like books?"

"I'm… starting to come around to them. Romances at least."

"Booker, your boat has a library!"

We were standing in a two story high, cedar paneled room that occupied a huge space in the center of the boat, between the master bedroom and the multiple guest rooms. It had plush red carpet, several chesterfield wing chairs—the brown leather, smoking-room kind—an antique telescope at the porthole, and wall to wall shelves that were *absolutely crammed* with books.

He grinned. "Do you like it?"

I gawped around me. "I do. I love it! But... but how?"

"When money is no object, things get done quickly." He looked oddly pleased with himself. "Yesterday, this was a ballroom. I think this is better."

Then his hand went to the back of his neck. "Just be warned, I have no idea what you'll find on the shelves. My agent tells me he purchased every English book in the city to fill this space."

I walked to a shelf. A dusty tome of International Law sat beside a Delta Force novel on one side, and the collected works of Dr. Seuss on the other. "Does it have the Kamasutra?"

He burst out laughing. "I've already asked. Unfortunately not."

CHAPTER TWO

We were on the top deck, a gentle breeze in our hair as we powered through the calm blue ocean. It was hot—a very pleasant change to the frigid conditions we'd just come from—and the water seemed very far below. "You know, this is more like a small city than a boat."

Booker laughed. "It was my second big purchase after I made my money, and the first real item I bought just for me. I'm glad you like it."

I pushed off the railing to dip my toe in the water of the Jacuzzi behind us. "Like it? I love it!" The water was cool in the tropical sun. "This water feels amazing by the way."

Booker's arms slipped around my waist from behind. "We could have a glass of champagne… watch the world sail by," he murmured. He kissed my neck. "Just you and me, without a care in the world."

I swiveled in his arms to face him. "Let's do it. Let's come back here after dinner."

His eyebrows rose. "Why wait? Why not now?"

I laughed. "Because I don't have any swimwear, that's why."

His shoes slipped off. "So?"

"But our clothes will get wet!"

He stepped into the spa, a dark line climbing his jeans as his foot lowered. He held an arm out to me. "So?" he said again.

"Booker! You'll ruin perfectly good clothes!"

His hand flashed out like a viper to catch my arm. "So?"

He began to pull me toward him.

"Don't you dare!"

"Oh, I dare, alright."

He was leaning back now, pulling me out over the edge of the water. I was beginning to overbalance. "Booker!" I squealed.

He laughed. "That's my name." Then he pulled me into the water.

I shrieked as we fell back together, collapsing with a splash. Booker came up laughing, and it was only a split second before I joined in too. I couldn't be angry. Booker was just too cheerful; too determined to see me happy.

I slapped him across the chest with a wet thunk. "You're incorrigible, you know that?"

He swept his hair back with a hand, clearing water from his face. "Come here and give me a kiss."

We met in the middle of the spa, kissing with a tang of chlorine on the lips and my hair plastered to my face, and it was the most wonderful moment of my life. I was with the man I loved, and we were on a boat in the middle of the ocean heading who knew where, and I didn't care. How far had I travelled to get to this spot? How much had changed?

I wanted to tell him what he meant to me. I wanted to tell him how much I appreciated what he was doing.

But with men, they said actions spoke louder than words. I would show him, instead. I straddled his lap in the water, kissing him again. Then I reached for his shirt, lifting it up with a coy smile. "What do you say we take this off?"

I could see his abs under the water, rippled and hard. Drawing the shirt off, his shoulder muscles flared for one glorious moment. It was like I was sharing the tub with my own private underwear model.

Speaking of which…

"Let's get these off too." I reached under the water to grasp at his belt and bit my lip. *I could feel him already, down there.*

I pulled the jeans from him, admiring his Calvin Kleins. The white material was just barely see-through under the water. I looked at the hard straining bulk beneath. "Happy to see me?"

He followed my gaze. "Would it be any other way sitting in a hot tub with you?"

I licked my lips and peeled his underwear off. His member sprang free, hard and incongruent in the formless waters of the tub.

My hands traced up its soft skin. I wanted to kiss it, to worship it; but under the water, I'd have to play a different game.

Everything was softer, more slippery when I gripped him. I began to stroke.

My fingers glided up and down his skin, cool and caressing in the hot water, working him leisurely, with no hurry, the swirl of the water a warm compliment to my strokes.

Before me, Booker had gone quiet. His hand reached up to caress my face as I worked. "Clara-"

"Shh," I said, cutting him off. "Just lie back and relax." I pushed him back with one hand as I stroked him with my other. He fought me, leaning in for a deep kiss before finally reclining against the Jacuzzi wall.

It felt naughty doing this. *On a boat, out in the open air.* Even though I knew no-one could see, the sunshine and the wind against my hair suggested differently. And it felt naughty servicing him; gaining my pleasure exclusively from his pleasure.

He began to breathe harder. I adjusted my grip and quickened my pace, my wrist emerging then disappearing under the water as splashes began to make the area bubble.

How must it feel? My hand slippery on his shaft, pulling then pushing at his most sensitive of nerves. My body pressed against his, the weight of my wet breasts in my shirt rough against his skin. The feel of my lips as I kissed him in a slow counterpoint to the ever quickening motion below.

He gave an involuntary buck of anticipation. Not long now, I could tell. Both hands grasped him and I pumped faster. The area between us became waves and bubbles that moved in time to the rhythm of my hands.

Booker groaned, then again, the sounds building in intensity as the pleasure inside him grew. One of his hands leapt to my shoulder, gripping it tight. "Clara!"

I could feel him within my hand. *I needed to see what I had done to him.* My motions ceased as he began to release, and the water cleared to reveal creamy spurts of fluid issuing from him wildly, to slow under the pressure of the water and begin to drift gently away. It was hypnotic: magical. I watched, spellbound, as his member jerked on display before me until his head collapsed against the spa's edge: the only thing now moving his chest; rising and falling heavily.

Suddenly I noticed, truly, where we were for the first time: in a spa on a superyacht sailing over the ocean, salt air and sunshine on our faces. It was a fantasy I had only ever dreamed about, but was now reality with Booker by my side.

And I noticed my clothing, wet upon my body, almost carnal in the way that it hugged my skin, appreciating my curves as I rose to stand in the water. It sucked at me, demanding that I satisfy the urge that had built as I satisfied Booker's.

It seemed he had the same idea. He pulled me to him, my summer dress floating around my waist as I sunk back into the water.

I shivered, delighting in the eddying current as he pushed my underwear aside. My arms went around his neck and we kissed, then one of his hands went to my hips and the other to his base and he guided me, slowly, upon him.

I groaned as I slid down his shaft, the feel of him inside me sending delicious shivers through my body. How could he generate such wonder and delight inside me?

Booker leaned back reaching for a button beside the spa. A low whir sounded. And then the spa began to bubble.

"Ohh." I could feel tickles all along my calves where spa jets hit and then trailed air upward. But between my legs, a different sensation was building. I could feel him inside me; our bases grinding together as we moved slowly upon each other, each tiny motion generating corresponding movements inside.

Being in the spa with Booker was like nothing I had ever experienced before. I was weightless, but anchored to him. We were exposed, and yet so intimately connected I could focus only on him. Liquid pools of pleasure were forming in my hips and thighs.

I needed this man. I needed him as much as his hard, firm member revealed he still needed me. I began to grind him in the water, kissing him as I did so, enjoying the feel of his hands as they roamed my breasts and back. Faster and faster we began to move, until the water was sloshing in the tub around us, exposing my thighs and then splashing up my back. The feeling inside me grew in time with the water, getting higher and more turbulent with each passing motion.

I closed my eyes, enjoying the sensation between my legs—a sensation that was now spreading to every inch of my body. Then I felt Booker shift, and suddenly the weight of my body was back. I opened my eyes to find him standing in the middle of the spa, lifting me while we were still connected, supporting me as he slid me up and down upon him. The abrupt change sent a whole new set of thrills through me. Thrills at his strength. Thrills at what the sudden heaviness did to the pressure of him inside. Thrills at being caught in his arms. I gasped, gripping his back, my vision spinning before I managed to focus with desperate eyes.

"I can feel it," I groaned. "I can feel it coming."

His response was a growl—a primal sound that sent shivers through me. Then he lay me over the edge of the spa and began to work me harder.

He drove into me as I lay on the decking, feet still in the water but body out. Now our motions were not heavy, but instead fast and sharp. Each collision as our bodies met sent shivers from my thighs to my brain. Each loud slap drove my pleasure higher. The liquid pools inside were starting to superheat. *Soon they must wash through my entire body.*

I began to moan, my hips flexing with him, then he lifted my legs high, to give him better access. The angle thrust him deeper; my eyes widened and my moans changed pitch. He raised my legs to his shoulders. I couldn't take it. I couldn't-

My loud moans changed to a single cry. "Booker!" And then the liquid pools burst inside, and pleasure raged through my body in a tidal wave of ecstasy that almost blacked me out. My cries set Booker off, too. He began to move sharply inside me. The feeling set me off once more, and suddenly we were sailing together on a sea of sensuous susurrations.

The feeling went on and on and on, until what felt like hours later he collapsed, panting, on top of me.

"Remind me to take a bath with you more often," he growled. "It's rather fun."

We both slid back into the water. I cuddled into his side, and we stayed there, in each other's company, minds drifting, until our breathing had slowed.

"Booker," I said hesitantly. My head lifted off his shoulder and I turned to him. "Can I ask you something?"

His head turned. "Anything."

There was something I'd been thinking about for a while. I didn't know how to say it… so what the heck, I was just going to come out with it.

"Booker, why are you leaving your wife?"

CHAPTER THREE

Booker sighed in the spa beside me, hand going to the back of his neck. "I was wondering when you'd ask."

"I'm sorry. It's just…"

Just… *what?* That I'd just had sex with a married man? That I needed to know the competition? *That I couldn't understand why anyone would want to give him up?*

I sighed. "If you don't want to tell me, that's okay."

"No. You deserve to know," he said. "It's just hard to know where to start."

I ran my hand through the water, playing with it. "How about you treat it like a book? Start at the beginning."

He chuckled. "Ok. Since you put it like that… Once upon a time, I guess we were in love. We married young, before I made my fortune. She was pretty, and she had a mean business sense."

He hesitated. "I became wealthy not long after, and that's when I first noticed the change. Suddenly it was all about the money. I'm sure jealousy was a part of it; I was the successful one, not her."

He shrugged, apologetic. "I know it's probably not what you want to hear, but I tried my hardest to fix things."

It was exactly what I needed to hear. I motioned for him to continue.

"The real trouble began the first time I used my new money."

"Did she think you were spending too much?" I murmured.

His laugh was short and sharp. "No. Especially since it was a gift for her."

A diamond ring perhaps. Or a car. "What was it?"

"An island."

I almost choked. "A what?"

"An island," he repeated. "I bought an island off the coast of Borneo. Pristine wilderness—the most amazing beaches, beautiful clear water, and a government corrupt enough to let us do whatever we wanted with it."

"Corrupt enough?"

His hand went to the back of his neck. "I was a different person back then, Clara. You have to understand, we bonded over business. My marriage was failing because my wife hadn't been as lucky as I was."

He looked out over the ocean. "The island was an anniversary present to my wife. We were going to build a resort on it; a way for her to make her own fortune, beside mine."

"What happened?" I asked, lost in his story. "Did the resort go up?"

He shook his head. "That's the problem. On our first trip there, I changed my mind. The land needed to be preserved, not destroyed. My wife disagreed."

I looked at him, confused.

"I guess this is where I admit that I have an ulterior motive for this trip." He indicated the horizon. "But it will be easier to show you. We should be there shortly."

CHAPTER FOUR

It was like we had sailed into a post card. Deep blue waters changed to turquoise in the late afternoon sunlight, and then suddenly they were aquamarine and we were dropping anchor on one of the most beautiful beaches I had ever seen. The white sand gave way to palm trees and then heavy jungle that rose to a peak on the island before us.

"This. This is your island?"

"Technically, it's my wife's. But she's only ever been here twice."

"It's beautiful!"

Booker nodded his agreement. "1600 acres of some of the most ecologically diverse wilderness on the planet, in an area twice as big as central park. Four species of monkey, two of which are endangered. 61 catalogued species of bird. The clouded leopard. There is a small population of natives on the-"

"Wait. Back up," I demanded, alarmed. "Leopard? As in the huge cat with lots of teeth?"

Booker's face darkened momentarily. "Not so huge. And also, not so many anymore. They're highly endangered."

"And natives?" I asked hesitantly.

He nodded. "An offshoot of the Dayak people in Borneo, I believe. But you won't see them. They don't like outsiders and have almost no contact with the outside world."

A text beeped from his pocket, and Booker pulled out his phone. His face brightened when he read the message. "You'll have to forgive me, but I have some work to do. Shall we meet for dinner at nine?"

* * *

I'd been in the library for two hours cataloguing Booker's collection when I heard a motor start up. It wasn't the *Leaf.* Had Booker taken the speedboat? I walked outside and in the darkening light followed a trail of barely visible wake until I saw the unlit shadow of the speedboat heading toward the shore. *What on earth was he doing?*

I ambled inside, content to go back to my books, until another thought occurred to me. *Why were the lights out on his boat? And why hadn't Booker told me he was leaving?*

I hesitated for only a moment before picking up the antique spyglass.

Booker had reached the shore by the time I found the boat again, a dark stain on the white beach. He leapt out, pulling a small shoe sized box with him. He looked to be heading toward the tree line.

I almost dropped the spyglass when my vision skimmed past Booker to a figure waiting in the shadows! Tall, with long, dark hair and a curvaceous figure.

A woman.

Booker approached her, there was what looked to be a brief conversation, and then she leapt into his arms and kissed him.

CHAPTER FIVE

I didn't mention the meeting when Booker got back.
Neither, more worryingly, did he. And so I told him I was
unwell; a half-baked excuse about bad chicken sticks that
he didn't question, but didn't believe, and then I avoided
him for the rest of the night on a boat so large that it
wasn't hard to do.

Was Booker cheating on me? I couldn't believe it. And
yet the evidence had been right there in the darkening
light. It hadn't been his wife—she was blonde, and anyway
they hated each other.

Perhaps this was the reason? All that story about the island
being the cause of their breakup. Maybe, perversely,
Booker had been telling the truth. I slipped into bed when
he began looking for me in earnest, then pretended I was
asleep when he finally found me. I couldn't deal with this
right now. In the morning, I'd confront him about my
fears.

* * *

I awoke eager to talk to Booker about what I had seen, convinced it must have all been a trick of the dying light. *But he was gone again when I awoke.*

I wandered aimlessly, the boat's toys bringing no joy. My mother had told me something once, words of wisdom I'd never forgotten. *Once a cheater, always a cheater.* But that couldn't be Booker. I knew him, didn't I?

To take my mind off things, I decided to make breakfast. I wasn't the world's greatest chef, but I could do a mean bacon and eggs when I tried. Food was a comfort thing for me—the act of eating, something that could anchor me briefly in the here and now. It was why I'd always carried a little weight after my own divorce those three or so years ago. It was why I'd started losing weight almost immediately after things worked out with Booker.

It was why I wanted to eat so bad again right now.

I was pulling bacon out of the fridge when I noticed Booker's phone. It was sitting on a bench in the galley kitchen, where he'd obviously left it when fixing his own breakfast. *Booker had received a text last night, shortly before saying he had 'work to do'.*

I reached out toward the phone, then pulled away. *I couldn't, could I?* Snooping was one of those things that you just didn't do in a trusting relationship.

I pulled eggs from the fridge next, and set them beside the bacon. *Next to the phone.*

But what if snooping could save a relationship? What if one little text could explain away all the doubts and fears… wouldn't it be worth it? My hand hovered, but I pulled away again. *No.*

My will broke halfway through doing the dishes. The phone had just been sitting there, watching me, and not even food had been able to stop me from thinking about what might be inside.

A phone number. A text message. An email explaining that the girl on the beach was secretly his long lost sister, or a cast member from Survivor….

I snatched up the phone before I could think about it—the trusting relationship had ended when Booker and that woman had met on the beach. I needed to know where I stood.

Most of the messages were as I'd expected—short, sharp ones to and from his wife, long sappy ones to and from me. I smiled when I read them, remembering the feelings behind what I'd written. Remembering what I'd felt when I'd read his replies. 'Two lovesick schoolkids' was the phrase Sandra at work had used. *She was just jealous.*

My smile faltered when I opened a short chain of texts to someone known only as 'L'.

> *It's Booker. I'm here.*
>
> *So I see.*
>
> *Have a package for you.*
>
> *The usual?*
>
> *How did you guess?*
>
> *Can't wait to wrap my lips around it ;)*
> *I'll come to you?*
>
> *No. Have company…*
> *Would rather she doesn't know.*
>
> *Obviously.*
>
> *Meet @ beach @ sunset.*
> *We can go to your place. B*

Well, there it was, as plain as day; so obvious that the tears had started before I even reached the end.

How could he do this to me? We were about to start a new life together! *Was I a front? Was I the excuse?* I had so many questions, but there was only one answer. I needed to get away.

Suddenly the boat felt dirty. Suddenly I felt dirty for being on it.

I'd cheated with a married man. The first time, perhaps I could be forgiven for. I hadn't known. But the second, and third, and fourth? I'd believed all the promises. I'd believed the look in his eyes. I'd allowed myself to finally be happy, for just one moment.... and this was what I got for it.

The phone dropped to the floor. I didn't bother to pick it up. Instead, I pulled a tube of cherry red lipstick from my back pocket, scrawled *It's Over* in huge letters on the fridge, and then strode angrily out the door.

CHAPTER SIX

I wasn't quite sure what I was doing. I only knew I didn't want to stay on this boat. I'd pushed a change of clothes and as many blurry books as I could fit into a backpack, and now I was standing at the Jet Ski launch, winching it angrily into the water as tears rolled down my cheeks.

Think he could cheat on me, did he? Think I was just going to roll over and take it?

The keys were in the ignition. I'd never ridden a Jet Ski before, but it couldn't be that hard. I gunned it and almost lost my balance before leaning into the wind and zipping toward the shore.

The breeze dried my eyes for the first time since I'd read that message. By the time I reached the shore I was thinking a little more rationally.

What was I actually going to do? I had no food, no water and no plan; just a hollow feeling in my stomach, and a heart that would never be the same again.

The Jet Ski was surprisingly heavy out of the water, but I managed to drag it high enough that it wouldn't float away. Then I walked up the most perfect sand I had ever failed to notice, toward the tree line just beyond.

Yep, there were the two sets of footprints, just like I'd seen. The last tiny, itsy bitsy spark of hope inside me died.

Maybe I could call for someone to pick me up? *Who, Sandra half a world away? Was she going to just fly over on her private helicopter?*

Well then maybe I'd just charter a plane to go home. *With what Clara? The overdrawn credit card, or the wallet you stupidly left on the boat?*

I didn't care—I'd find a way. The important thing was that I was off the boat and never had to see him again.

The thought hit me harder than I could have ever thought possible. Never feel his warm embrace. Never giggle at the tickle of his breath on my neck. Never snuggle into his arms after a night of passionate sex.

Why did he have to be like this? Why couldn't he just be happy with me?

I looked down at myself, barefoot in the sand. At the dimples in my legs and the short stubby toes...

No. I couldn't think like that. This was Booker's fault, not mine. I stood, and began to walk down the beach, away from this life and toward another.

* * *

I was two coves along when I stopped walking; far enough away from the boat that I could no longer see it. The tears had started and gone again, and now I was just walking, feet in the sand, with nowhere in particular to go. Maybe I'd have to go back to the boat, I didn't know. But for now it was good just to be away from everything, to be completely surrounded by nature.

I'd opened my bag earlier, thinking that a book might help me escape for a while. No such luck—I had children's books, a used car guide and a dictionary, but not a romance in sight. I really should have looked at what I was packing.

I was thirsty now. Probably should have packed some water, too. I moved to the shade of a palm tree. Funny thing about a deserted island—I hadn't stopped to think that 'deserted' also meant no vending machines.

I thought for a moment. What would that guy, Bear Grylls, do on that survival show? Hmm—I wasn't desperate enough to drink my own urine *quite yet*. Perhaps there was a creek nearby? All these trees must get their water somehow.

Tentatively, I left the beach, walking inland. There was an animal track of some kind. They usually led to water, right?

The jungle was cool after the heat of the beach. A different kind of quiet—no longer the gentle lapping of waves, but the chirps of birds and creak of trees instead. Soon it got cool enough that I began to shiver. I pulled a shawl over my shoulders.

A noise in the distance made my head turn. *A branch falling, perhaps*. Actually, it was kind of spooky here in the deep gloom of the jungle.

I stopped. There was that sound again—but closer. Something skittered from the path ahead.

I'd never been camping. Not really. Roughing it for me was a cabin with an outhouse and two ply toilet paper.

What the fudge was I doing out here? I suddenly thought about where I was. *A deserted island with leopards, and monkeys*. Monkeys could be vicious—what if they weren't like *Curious George* at all, but rather big savage beasts that were all bloodshot eyes and sharp teeth? Chimpanzees were the worst, I'd heard—they ripped apart intruders with their bare hands!

Then I had another thought. There was a tribe on this island. Savages—headhunters, for all I knew. And they didn't like strangers. How easy it could be for me to be speared or eaten or even just break a bone and *never, ever be found again.*

Maybe I should head back to the shore...

Yes. Good idea. Before that overactive imagination of mine started scaring the fudge out of me. I turned to set off back down the path I had just walked...

...And there, blocking the path with spear in hand, was one of the savages.

CHAPTER SEVEN

Booker found me late that afternoon, a look of panic on his face and a pistol on his hip.

I looked up from the book I was reading, several small children in my lap. "You're not welcome here."

He looked at me, relief washing across his features. "Thank God I've found you."

"I appreciate your concern," I said. "I'm fine."

More than fine, actually. After a standoff where I think my scream frightened them more than they frightened me, one of the villagers had said something to me in a language that I didn't understand. I'd shaken my head, moving to walk away, to which the villagers had leveled their spears at me. I'd remained frozen to the spot until a young child arrived who could speak English. The child's name was Ford, which he proudly explained was after a car he had never seen, and then in an oddly British accent he had told me that outsiders weren't allowed on this island, and that I'd have to leave.

I'd promptly burst into tears, saying I wished I could, leaving the adults with confused expressions on their faces.

After a moment, Ford had crossed the path between us to give me a hug. Then he'd said something to the Elders, and after a brief discussion I'd ended up here—drinking some sort of herbal tea and reading books to an ever growing gaggle of children.

"If you don't mind Booker, I have to get back to reading *Thomas the Tank Engine*. It's rather harder than you'd imagine when these children have never seen a train before. You can see yourself out."

Booker shook his head. "Clara, what's going on? I found the note on the fridge, and then... what did I do?"

The book shut with a clap, prompting several young cries of outrage. "Seriously?" I asked. "You have to ask me that? You tell me things will be different, that you're getting divorced, and then the first moment you get, you go behind my back and kiss another woman?"

"Clara, I never-"

"Don't even try, Booker. I saw you on the beach with that woman. Who is she? Your other lover? Some random holiday fling because you got bored with me so quickly?" I was trying so hard to keep my voice level in front of the children that the words came out between gritted teeth. "Do you really care so little about me that you would do that?"

Booker's hand went to the back of his neck. "Actually, it's because I care about you that I didn't want to tell you."

"You were just going to keep her a secret?"

He shook his head. "No, it's not like that at all. I have a confession Clara. We didn't just come here for a holiday. I didn't want to tell you, but..."

I looked at him. One of the children reached up to wipe at a tear as it trickled down my cheek.

He sighed, then motioned to the forest line some 30 paces distant. A shadow detached itself and a woman walked toward me. The woman I had seen from the boat.

"Booker. What's she doing here?"

The woman strode across the distance between us; camouflage paint crisscrossing the parts of her body that khaki pants and black singlet failed to cover. Her long dark hair was caught in a battered baseball cap. Across one arm rested a long, blackened automatic weapon.

Gently, I lifted the children off my lap, motioning them behind me.

"Booker…"

I tried to hold the children back, but suddenly they ran to the woman. She laughed, scooping them up to ruffle their hair.

"Clara, I'd like you to meet Leena."

* * *

Leena offered me her hand. "How do you do?" she said in a British accent. "It's such a pleasure to finally meet you— not often I get to talk in the Queen's language anymore."

What I had previously thought was paint on her arms were actually tattoos. Long, intricate whorls that wound from her wrist all the way up her arms to the side of her neck, stopping at her jawline. Her face was the only part of her actually painted. She had full lips and dark, piercing eyes that reminded me of a panther's—beautiful, but dangerous even to look at, lest she notice and return your stare.

"Um…" The children hopped down to run rings around us as I got to my feet and shook a hand that felt like it could break me. "Hi?"

"I met Lenz several years ago," Booker said. "She was ex-SAS, fed up with doing the government's dirty work and looking to get off the grid for a while. I had a solution which I thought she might be interested in. We've been good friends ever since."

"That solution. It involved…" I looked between the two of them.

Leena got it first. She burst out laughing. "Sorry—no offense, but I never mix business with *that* kind of pleasure."

"Then what was the kiss on the beach?" I asked hotly. I didn't care whether she could crush me like a twig—I knew what I'd seen. "And why all the secrecy?"

"The kiss?" asked Booker, confused. Then his eyes cleared. "You must mean the present I brought her— Leena has a weakness for cigars." He walked toward me, but I pulled away.

"And why would you be giving her cigars? Is her last name Lewinsky?"

Booker coughed. "Lenz *does* work for me. But not like that."

Leena looked to Booker. "I still don't think this is a good idea Boss."

Booker turned to her and shook his head. "The alternative is worse. Without Clara, none of this matters." Then he turned to me. "Clara, I said that my wife had been to this island twice. Once, just after I bought it for her, when we visited together."

He paused. "The second time, she came alone. To… to hunt."

"To what?"

"My wife… well, unlimited wealth and unlimited time did something to her. Her mind began to twist. It started with small things—ordering people around, dropping a bottle just to make the maids clean up after her. But it grew. She began to buy fur coats. And then ivory, for no other reason than the fact that other people with less money couldn't. I blew my top when I found out."

He went silent for a moment. "Then she started taking the holidays," he continued.

"Without you?"

"I was busy—my own fault, not hers. Too much time with my head in the books, one of the reasons I grew away from them for so long. So I was happy to let her have her little vacations, always just a few days, always to find her in a better mood when she returned."

His fists clenched. "Happy, until I found out where she was going. Canada, Spain, *Africa*. Clara," he said. "They were hunting safaris."

A chill ran through me. "Hunting?"

"Slaughtering animals for sport. Just like that Minnesota dentist did to that famous lion in Zimbabwe."

"Cecil the Lion," I whispered horrified. I'd seen the pictures on the news, of the poor animal lying bloody on the ground, eyes glazed and tongue out. "That's barbaric."

Booker nodded, his face a mask of barely controlled rage. "And when the thrill of legal hunting wasn't enough, my wife remembered somewhere that she had seen an animal so rare there were only a few left in the wild. And she remembered that she owned the land it lived on."

His fists clenched. "We separated the day I found out, when she walked into the house with a leopard pelt around her neck, and told me she was going to build a hunting reserve here; a way for the wealthy to get the ultimate thrill—hunting a creature to extinction."

He paused. "That was three years ago."

"What happened?" I asked breathlessly.

Booker nodded to Leena. "She came along. She wanted to go off grid. I needed someone 'unofficial' to stop that Lodge ever being built."

"You kill people?" I asked, horrified.

She shook her head. "No. Booker won't let me do that. But I sabotage equipment—make sure every time someone lands here, they go home packing. No construction company will touch the place—they think it's a guerilla group working in the area."

Booker nodded. "I've been paying off the government to keep a blind eye. But with the end of my funds-"

"You won't be able to keep up the bribes," I said.

Booker nodded again. "Lenz has said she would work for free, but it's too dangerous. When they stop taking my money, they'll start taking my wife's, and her orders will be to shoot to kill."

I looked from one to the other. "So... what now?"

Booker's grin became a rictus snarl. "We go out with a bang."

* * *

Son of a Biscuit. I'd been such a fool. I didn't deserve a man like Booker, who saw a crazed note scrawled across a fridge and then didn't just turn away, but strode into the jungle to find me and make it alright again.

I burst into tears—I'd done a lot of that lately, but this time they were tears of shame.

Booker strode toward me; wrapping my body in those broad, strong arms of his, kissing the top of my head. "Shh, it's ok."

I shook my head in his arms. "It's not. Every time I think I'm happy, I go imagining the worst. Every time you do nothing but show how much of a good man you are, I go threatening to leave you."

He held me at arm's length. "You're worth it," was all he said. Then he wrapped me in his arms until my tears ended.

I became aware of Leena, arms crossed, chewing a leaf and leaning against a post nearby. "I'm so sorry you had to see that."

Leena grinned. "Don't mind me. This is a better soap than *East Enders.*"

I looked at her, confused.

"Sorry," she said. "I forgot you're American. Think *The Bold and the Beautiful*, but with cups of tea."

I giggled, Booker grinned, and suddenly the whole world was ok again.

Leena pulled a map from one of her pockets, and Booker explained what he and Leena had been doing. It wasn't legal, which is why he hadn't wanted me involved—

he knew how I felt about breaking rules. He also wanted me innocent, in case things went wrong.

They were planning a raid. This island was larger than the others, but several around it were more developed. On one of them, Leena had noticed construction equipment massing. Her guess was that Booker's wife was waiting for the divorce papers before sending a team to bulldoze the south side of the island and build her Hunting Lodge.

Without Booker's interference, the workers would have an armed government guard. And the remaining animal population wouldn't have a chance.

Booker and Leena were going to hit them first. It would be dangerous, but blowing the compound where his wife's equipment was kept would protect the animals for a few more months.

"What happens after that?" I asked.

Booker looked to Leena, then back to me. And he suddenly became quiet. "I made my choice," he said. "And I chose you."

CHAPTER EIGHT

It wasn't how I'd imagined our vacation to play out. Somewhere in the back of my mind I'd imagined tropical beaches, yes, but tropical beaches with a backdrop of resorts behind, and margaritas by the pool. The only five stars I'd seen since we'd arrived had been the arms on a *Phylum Echinodermata*, otherwise known as the common starfish.

Still, somehow, this was better. The tranquility of those mornings after Booker found me, when he'd roll over and nudge me. I'd stumble grudgingly from bed to survey a view that took my breath away.

And serene evenings, when we'd sit in the spa or on deckchairs with a cocktail and watch nature's most perfect of movies—an orange sky fading slowly to indigo, the distant screech of monkeys and birds echoing over the water as the island's nocturnal population awoke.

The only blemish would be after lunch, when we'd board Booker's speedboat and motor toward the shore; Booker dropping me off with a kiss, Leena grunting a hello as we changed places.

It wasn't him motoring off with another woman that was the problem. Relationships were about trust, and I'd already failed that test once on this vacation. I wasn't going to do that again.

And it wasn't that I couldn't go with them. I understood Booker's motives for keeping me out of things. This was something he had to do, and besides, I was a librarian who had lived in a city all her life—I had absolutely nothing I could contribute.

Rather, my discomfort came from where Booker and Leena were going—what they were planning on doing. They were going to break the law, and that didn't sit well with me.

We'd argued about it, that evening he'd found me, standing on the shore as the stars came out. But Booker had simply pointed to the untouched sand beneath us and the forest at our backs, and held his fingers to his lips. I'd quieted, listening to the sounds of the jungle. Birds chirping, and then a monkey's chatter. And somewhere in the distance, the roar of one of the last great cats.

I hadn't had an answer for him after that. What was any rule if it meant this forest would one day be silent?

In a way, he was doing it all for me. That was the bittersweet point of it all. Me, a woman who had lived her life following the rules, now the one causing them to be broken. If I hadn't come along, Booker wouldn't be in this situation. He might be divorced, yes, but it would have been on his own terms, this island transferred to him as part of the deal.

The solution was simple. All we had to do was break up. *Simple, but impossible.* And while his actions might slow things for a while, they wouldn't last forever. Sooner or later, this island would have hunters on it. It was our relationship, ultimately, that had doomed it.

There had to be another way. A way to stop the ex-wife. *A way to protect the island.*

Each day, as I trudged the beach, the problem looped in my mind. I'd walk sands of pure white; between emerald green forest and turquoise blue sea, and not see a thing but the problem in my head.

Not until I reached the second cove, that is. Then I'd hear a youthful shout, and my head would snap up, and a smile would spring to my face as suddenly cries began to echo down the beach ahead of me. A swarm of little figures would start racing barefoot across the sand, their excited laughter growing louder as they approached, until finally they'd surround me with a wall of noise and animated bodies, and all my worries would wash away.

When I reached the village I'd be kissed by the elders and greeted with food, the children running back and forth with an excess of energy until I sat down. They'd gather in a circle and sit excitedly too. Then slowly, tantalizingly, I'd pull a book from my bag.

By chance, a number of books purchased by Booker's agent for the library had been for younger readers; an occurrence that I suspected owed more to the need to fill shelves in the large space than anything else.

Part of my job as a librarian back home had been story time sessions with younger children. I'd enjoyed it there, but this… this was something else entirely. Before my arrival, the village had owned just three books—a battered copy of something in French that nobody could read, a car manual that looked to be from the 1920s, and the village's most prized possession, an alphabet picture book that had such riveting lines as *A is for Apple*, and *B is for Bear*.

It was Leena who had taught the young ones to speak, but her lessons had been all discipline and purpose—a means through which she could communicate with the elders. She'd had no time for the joy of stories, only for practical commands.

I'd taken it upon myself to teach them the joy that words could create, the magic in a story. The shared world that a book could bring.

Each book I pulled from my bag was an object of treasure. Not just a story, but a window into a faraway land; an education about the world beyond this small, green island. Today, we were reading *Oh, the Places You'll Go! By Dr. Seuss.*

> *You have brains in your head.*
> *You have feet in your shoes.*
> *You can steer yourself*
> *any direction you choose.*
> *You're on your own. And you know what you know.*
> *And YOU are the one who'll decide where to go.*

It was a magical book, and by the time I had finished even the adults were standing around, one of the children translating me word for word as I read. It was met with a round of applause when I finished. The children called for me to read it again.

I laughed, about to acquiesce, when soft words quieted the village. I paused, searching for the voice that had spoken.

More soft words, and the crowd parted. An elder was walking forward, his steps measured by the tap of a cane in his right hand. He had the long earlobes of the very old and ribs showed across his bare chest, but his stride was firm. He said something in the local dialect to Ford.

The child listened, then with a nod turned to me. "He says it is time."

I looked from him to the old man. "Time for what?"

The elder said something else to the child.

"To read the words," the young boy translated. He pulled me to my feet. "He says you have to come."

* * *

We walked through the village—the elder, Ford and I, the path lined on either side by villagers. Mothers stood with their children, the youngest still suckling at the breast. Warriors stood by their sides. It felt like we were walking with an honor guard as we passed through them and into the jungle beyond.

It was the first time I'd truly left the safety of the beach since that initial frightening foray. The first time I had truly lost sight of civilization.

"Ford, can you ask the elder where we are going?"

The elder seemed to understand the tone of my enquiry. He shook his head, talking briefly to the young boy.

"He says it is important for you to see this, Wordkeeper."

"Wordkeeper?"

"Person who keeps words," he said simply. Then he gestured toward the elder, as if that would help. "Like him."

I didn't understand. *Was the old man a librarian? Did he keep the village's three books?*

Then it clicked. Many tribes passed their knowledge by word of mouth; the shaman or lore master of the village bearing the heavy responsibility of remembering that community's history and laws. He thought I was something similar.

I opened my mouth to refute him but then stopped. What were librarians, if not word keepers for a different medium?

Ford talked briefly to the elder, as if questioning something. The elder nodded once, sharply.

"What did you ask him?"

The boy took my hand. "You must be special. You're the first outsider to ever see this place."

A shiver ran up my spine, and I looked anew around me. My time in the village had taught me to love this island. I no longer feared the jungle. Instead… maybe it was the elder's words, but there was something magical about this place. Primordial. Beautiful.

My heart grew heavy. *And it was all going to be destroyed.*
"Ford…"

"Yes?"

I shook my head. How could I tell a young boy something like that? How could I tell an old man that had lived here all his life that this was going to change? Because it wouldn't just be the animals that suffered. If Booker's wife was anything like what I imagined, this village would be the first to go—they would be the only opposition left on the island, the only witnesses to her crimes.

There must be a way. There must be something I could do. Something more than just giving Booker my encouragement and staying out of Leena's way.

We followed a clear brook that babbled beneath the trees and birdcalls for 20 minutes, picking our way slowly down a track beside the water. It was pleasant work, the pace slow to account for the elder. But then we turned suddenly at a place marked only by an ancient tree.

"Ford, why are we leaving the track?"

"This place is protected by our people. We leave no tracks so that it might be preserved."

"Ford, where are we going?"

The young boy shook his head with a motion too old for such a youthful body. "Patience, Wordkeeper."

The forest began to slope uphill; we walked at a leisurely pace, the old man surprisingly agile with his cane, simply slow. He had muscles like string across his arms and legs, but they were taught and wiry, and it occurred to me to wonder why someone so fit should move at a pace just measured enough to be comfortable for myself. I turned to him, but he caught my eye and winked.

"We have time," the young boy translated.

I laughed. I was being concerned for him when, all this time, he'd been looking after me! These people really were the sweetest—like instant family. *Family that was going to be broken-*

The old man lifted his cane to point ahead, interrupting my train of thought. A huge tumble of boulders, some twice as big as me, lay before a sheer wall that rose above the trees. The forest stopped where the rocks began, opening the area to surprising but welcome sunlight.

I scrambled to the top of a smaller pile of scree, panting slightly. We'd been going comfortably, but we'd still climbed a fair way. I could see the village over the top of the jungle below us and the *Leaf* two bays beyond. This must be the start of the peak I had been able to see from the boat; the one that dominated most of the island.

"Where now?" I asked. "Up?"

Please don't let it be up. We were high enough already thank-you-very-much.

The elder laughed as my face blanched. Then he skipped around a huge boulder ahead and disappeared.

I followed, cautiously.

Oh wow. A cave opened into the side of the cliff, so deep that I couldn't see where it ended. The old man beckoned, a toothy smile on his face, and Ford took my hand. "Come. This is what you need to see."

This close, a small track was visible leading inside, and we followed it, stopping at the edge of darkness where the sunlight failed.

"It's lovely. But... why? What do you need me to do?" I asked, confused. I was no cave specialist capable of exploring its dark depths. I was no photographer capable of capturing its beauty.

The old man said something to Ford, and the child removed a cheap, battered plastic torch from his pocket. He handed it to the old man.

The elder began to speak to me. I looked to Ford.

"We show you this, Keeper of Words, so that you may record these too," he said, face screwed up in concentration. "The first words."

The elder switched on the torch. I looked to the wall.

And I gasped. Around me, the yellowed limestone sprang into sight, stretching away into the distance. And upon it, images. Reds, browns and blacks—artificial to walls but somehow still a part of them—cave paintings that looked so old their meaning should be forgotten. I moved closer. There was a hand. And there… the outline of a person. A hunting scene, the conclusion to which disappeared into the shadows.

"This… what is this?"

The old man spoke.

"He says it is the history of our people," said Ford. "From the time of our ancestors until today, our magic men have come to this cave to read the walls, learn of our past and record our knowledge."

The old man tapped on his cane, and spoke again.

"When he was young, he says he came here too," said Ford. "He says he is embarrassed to say the thing he was fascinated with wasn't as traditional as most."

I walked to where the old man was gesturing to the opposite wall. I'd missed it on the way in, but there was a drawing here too, about the size of a small dog, it's colors richer than those deeper in the cave. It was vaguely recognizable; a black box-like top with visored hood, sitting upon round, spoked wheels.

"Is that… a car?" It looked as if the artist had seen a picture of a Model –T Ford and then tried to recreate it from memory.

The old man nodded when Ford translated, and then spoke rapidly.

"A missionary came here once. He had a picture in a book. I thought it was the most wonderful thing."

I looked from the car back into the caves. Modern conveniences that gave way to things more ancient. Animals. Hunts. *Gods.*

"How far back does this go?" I asked in wonder.

Ford struggled to provide an answer. "I am sorry; I do not know the word in your language. Very big distance.

Almost through mountain. The elder tells the story that our people first arrived by foot, not boat."

How old must this cave be? How long had this village—this tribe—been here in unbroken settlement? *They arrived when this island was still a part of the mainland. Before it broke off.*

The old man spoke again.

"He asks you to witness our history," the young boy said. "He said that the times are changing too fast, that the guardians of the island may not be able to preserve it for much longer."

Was he talking about Booker and Leena?

"As a keeper of words, you must ensure we are not forgotten." The young boy hesitated, then added something of his own. "It is important, the past," he said, eyes too serious for such a small face. "For without it, we have nothing to guide our future."

CHAPTER NINE

Nothing to guide *our future...*

The words haunted me, playing over and over in my mind after I returned to the boat that evening. Booker had left a Jet Ski on the beach for me, he must be still working.

There was something about that child's words—the germ of an idea that might help the village. *But what?*

It was a cave, yes? So maybe they could hide the animals there? I dismissed the idea as stupid. Maybe the village could hide there, or Booker and Leena, to launch their...

Booker and Leena—*I'd almost forgotten!*

I ducked into the galley and five minutes later was walking with three mugs of steaming hot coffee up to the bridge. "How go the preparations?"

Booker rolled up the map that he and Leena had been hunched over, then strode over to kiss me deeply—it was the first time we'd seen each other since that morning. "Fine," he said, eyes avoiding mine. "Just... you know, looking at our options."

I rolled my eyes, handing out the mugs. "Seriously Booker, it's very sweet that you're trying to keep me out of this, but I know tomorrow's the big day."

Leena almost choked on her coffee. "Told you she'd figure it out."

Booker's eyebrows had risen, but I could see a little crinkle of pride there too. "Why do you say that?"

I crossed my arms. "I don't know—something about the five crates of explosives I found in the hold this morning labelled 'sugar' was my first clue. You're lucky I'm not a baker!"

Booker grinned, then took a huge gulp from his mug. "The coffee is great, by the way."

"Thank you. Second," I said, refusing to be thrown off topic. "No-one tells their partner *a day in advance* that they'll be going for a jog before daylight the following morning. You really should have thought of a better excuse about why you're waking up early tomorrow."

He had the decency to look ashamed even as Leena chuckled. His hand went to the back of his head. "Would you believe I've had a sudden urge to get fit?"

"I believe you're about to do something very dangerous tomorrow, and it isn't exercise." I began to tap my foot. "Out with it, buster."

He winced, then kissed me again. "I do love you, you know that right?"

"Yes. Now spill it."

He sighed, then rolled his map back out. "Look, I'm serious about not getting you involved in this, but I guess you do have a right to know what we're going to do, in case things escalate."

"Escalate?"

Booker looked to Leena. "We think my wife might have worked out what's been going on here—the fact that guerilla activity only ever started after she wanted to set up a hunting lodge. The fact that she most likely knows I'm here now." He sighed. "Leena's last scout of the camp has come back... worrying."

I looked to the tattooed woman before me.

"Armed guards at every entrance," she said. "And they've begun constructing floodlight towers. Once they're up, we won't have a chance. It's now or never."

"What's the plan?"

"Nothing fancy. We sneak in under cover of darkness, rig their stores with explosive, get out, and blow it."

"What about the guards?"

"That's why there are two of us. While Lenz rigs the stuff to blow, I'll create a distraction." He patted the handgun on his hip. "I'll make myself seen; fire a couple of shots and then head for the beach, leading them away."

"But isn't that dangerous?" I asked.

He shrugged. "It is—any one of a number of things could go wrong. I could trip, the Jet Skis might not start... I could get shot. But I'd rather risk my life than become a murderer." His brows furrowed. "Those guards are locals, Clara. They're not the bad guys, just people trying to put food on the table for their families."

He moved to me. "If anything happens, I've made provisions to get you back to America. There's a helicopter on standby not far from here, and then a plane waiting to take you home."

He paused. "And if local authorities are an issue, there's also $50,000 in unmarked bills in the safe within the master bedroom." He gave me a wink. "Type your name into the keypad on your phone, and the number that comes up will be the code."

I wasn't quite sure what to say. This had all just become so real. Booker could get hurt... or killed.

"Booker..."

He kissed me again. "I know. But it has to be done. If you can think of anything better, I'm happy to hear it—otherwise, we leave before dawn."

CHAPTER TEN

It was so frustrating!

I paced the boat, unable to sleep without Booker in the bed, unable to do anything except worry about what would happen just a few short hours from now. It was 11:30pm, Booker might not survive the next day, and there was not one thing I could do about it.

I was a librarian for heaven's sake! I wasn't a fighter, or a doctor, or anything at all that could be of any help. I was going crazy with worry.

I could speed read, when I wanted to. And I was one heck of a researcher—give me a university assignment, and I could give the student the four books she would need to ace it in under five minutes. But none of that felt very helpful right now. I'd never felt so inadequate in my whole life. There was literally nothing I could do.

A sudden thought hit me. *Or was there?*

I turned on a hunch, and ran toward the library.

* * *

There *was* something I could do. I wasn't sure quite what it was yet, but it had been niggling around the edges of my brain all day, demanding attention but then hiding each time I got close. It had something to do with that cave. Something my thoughts about research had sparked again.

Booker's last minute request for a library had turned out to be a blessing. It was horribly short on romance, but what it didn't have in unrequited love, it made up for in esoteric books about everything and anything.

I pulled book after book from the shelf—anything I thought might be helpful. There were books on prehistoric man, and even one on cave art—I put that on the top of the pile. Beside it I created another pile on endangered species. I built pile after pile on the library floor, cataloguing it as I went. By the time I was done, more than a quarter of the library lay at my feet. A big ask for any normal reader, but I was a librarian. Reading wasn't just a skill. For me, it was an art form.

I began at the obvious choice first—a 2005 second hand copy of Jean Clottes' *Cave Art*—one of the world's leading tomes on cave paintings. I flicked through the pages quickly. Paintings ranged from 11,000 to 35,000 years old, mostly European. I suspected that the paintings in the island's cave might be somewhere between those ages, if what Ford had said was correct. But how would that stop hunters?

I moved to a 1937 book titled *The Negritos of Malaya*. It was of interest because an anthropologist had visited Malaysia in the early 1920s, where he had found a tribe that still used cave paintings just like the Dayak did, to tell their history. The book was a dry read, but it gave me hope—there was something here, if I could just tie it all together!

I looked at my watch, and then picked up the next book in the pile, a short hardcover on the geological history of the area. It was 12am. I didn't have much time left.

* * *

I threw another book to the side in frustration, for once not caring about the state it landed in. It was 5am, I'd been up all night, I'd read almost every book in this useless library, and I'd still come up with nothing!

Words were beginning to swim across the pages I was reading. Maybe I should just go to bed. Not that I would be able to sleep—Booker would be leaving shortly.

I flicked through another book without really looking, then threw it down despondently. What was the use? Unless Booker stapled an encyclopedia to his body, words could never stop a bullet. The pen could not be mightier than the-

Wait.

Amidst the despair, the spark that I'd been chasing reared its head once more. What had I just been thinking about? Cave paintings, yes… but what else.

My eyes drifted to a shelf that had only one book left. A thick, dusty old tome of International Law. *The same size as an encyclopedia.* I hadn't even bothered to pull it down before—Booker's wife was clearly breaking the law hunting animals here, and Booker himself had proven that local authorities could be bought for the right price. But maybe… *yes.* That spark had flared again. Maybe there was something else within its pages that might be of use.

I leapt for the volume, finger flying down the index.

International Legal Framework? *No.*

Repatriation of Movable Cultural Heritage? *No*

World-

"Yes!" I snapped the book shut, leaping to my feet with a prayer that I wouldn't be too late. "Booker! Wait!"

CHAPTER ELEVEN

Leena was already in the speedboat when I reached the outer deck, panting. "Wait!"

"Clara!" Booker said, surprised, pausing on the ladder. "I thought you were asleep, I didn't want to wake you.

"Booker, you have to wait."

He climbed back up. "I'm so glad I get to say good-"

"Stop," I cut him off. "That's not why I'm here. You don't have to say goodbye."

His face clouded. "I love you baby. And that's why I won't let you come. We've already spoken about this-"

"No," I cut him off again. "Just listen to me."

In the boat, Leena hissed with impatience. "We don't have time for this—we need to go now, or we lose the dark."

Booker's hand went to the railing once more. "Clara. This is something I have to do. I'll be home in time for breakfast, I promise."

"Booker, please. *If you love me.* Stop and listen."

Booker's hands froze.

"Booker," Leena hissed again. "We need to leave, now!"

Booker looked to the boat. Then he looked to me.

And then he climbed back up the ladder.

* * *

Leena and Booker were both standing before me now. Leena with her dark tattoos and face paint, Booker in dark clothes himself, his face smeared with grease but eyes resolute. Leena opened her mouth to speak, but Booker held up a hand.

"Clara knows how important this is to me. And she knows our timeframes," he said firmly. "I know it's something important that she's got to say. What is it Sheets? What did you discover?"

I held the book in front of me. "I've been in the library doing research. And I've found something. Something that might mean you don't have to go through with this."

I thrust the book toward him, thumb still in the page I wanted him to read. "Sections three and five."

Booker scanned the page briefly, and then began to read out loud. "Section three. To exhibit an important interchange of human values, over a span of time or within a cultural area of the world, on developments in architecture or technology, monumental arts, town-planning or landscape design."

He scratched his head, frowning. "Section five. To be an outstanding example of a traditional human settlement, land-use, or sea-use which is representative of a culture, or human interaction with the environment especially when it has become vulnerable under the impact of irreversible change." He looked at me. "Clara, what is this?"

I looked between Booker and Leena. "They're criteria for selection."

"For?"

I drew a deep breath. "World Heritage Listing."

Booker frowned again. "This island is beautiful, but I don't think it qualifies. Interchange of human values? Examples of human settlement? There are villagers here… what are you getting at?"

"Booker. I didn't tell you earlier because you were occupied." I shrugged. "And to be quite honest, I hadn't quite processed what I'd seen myself. But the villagers here, they showed me something."

Leena looked up, frowning. "The cave?"

"You've seen it?"

She shook her head. "I've heard of it. All I know is it's where they do initiations, or something."

I grasped Booker's hands. "It's so much more than that. Booker, the walls are painted."

He cocked his head. "Like… cave paintings?"

"Yes! But not just a couple. Thousands and thousands, stretching all the way into the mountain."

"And… you think this qualifies for World Heritage Listing?"

I nodded. "Booker, the elder of this village told me today that people have lived on this island since it was a part of the mainland. I've checked, and that's almost 15,000 years ago. And those caves are an *unbroken line* of art from then until present day—the people of the past speaking to the future in language written on the walls. It's got to be the most important discovery of the century!"

"Definitely World Heritage quality," Booker mused, understanding finally dawning in his eyes.

"But how does this help us?" Leena asked, perplexed.

It was Booker that answered. "The World Heritage Organization is a body beyond local politics. They can't be bribed, and their whole purpose is to protect. If we tell them about this, teams will have to investigate. They'll list the island as a heritage area, and they'll have the manpower to enforce it. My wife won't be able to hunt here—ever again."

"Even better," I added, "is that people are going to want to study this—with the village's permission. And people on the island with cameras and links to the outside world will mean that even if your wife does want to hunt illegally, she'll be too afraid to. The media attention would ruin her! You saw what happened to that dentist after he shot Cecil the Lion!"

Booker's arms slipped around my waist. "I think you've done it, Clara. We'd have to talk to the village, ask their permission, but I think you might just have saved the island. How on earth did you discover this?"

I grinned. "I'm a librarian, remember? Research is my forte—and protecting information is my job."

CHAPTER TWELVE

The water lapped gently on the shores as we walked hand in hand in the starlight along the beach. It had only been one week since the discovery that had changed this island, but so much had already happened.

The villagers had been hesitant at first. But they had trusted me—enough to listen to the reasons behind what we wanted to do. Enough to sit down and debate between themselves the best course of action. In the end, they had agreed, the elder who had first shown me the caves wrapping me in a warm hug, tears of thanks streaming down his cheeks. Ford hadn't needed to translate his words then—I'd understood.

World Heritage Listing meant more than just protecting endangered species. It meant protecting a way of life for the villagers too—big development would never be able to touch this island.

The village would even benefit! I'd found a book on ecotourism which the elder was very interested in getting translated; as soon as he could pry Ford away from Booker that is—the little boy followed him everywhere.

Booker had flown UNESCO out the day after the village made their decision. They'd been welcomed with a local ceremony, had asked the elders for permission to see the sacred site and since then had been busy with a whirlwind of investigations and communications—the find had set the scientific community abuzz with interest. The village wasn't yet taking media, but that would come with time—when they found their own balance between the old and new.

The best part for me had been Booker's wife. She was furious! And there was nothing she could do. World heritage listing couldn't take the property away from her, but it could prevent '*any activity that was likely to have a significant impact on matters of national environmental significance.*' Poor spoiled little baby…

"Tomorrow's our last day," I said softly as we walked barefoot along the sand, waves lapping at our feet. The stars were bright overhead, bathing the entire beach in a soft white glow.

Booker sighed. "Back to reality—my wife texted me earlier. She's sick of waiting, she wants those divorce papers signed."

I snuggled into his side. "Maybe there's some way we can beat her at this, too?"

He shook his head. "All the research in the world won't make that contract null and void. If I want to stay with you, I give it all up. That's the deal."

"Maybe we could keep this a secret?"

Booker shook his head. "You already know how I feel about that. It won't work." He stopped, feet in the water, and turned to me. "Clara, money is just that—money. If I didn't already believe it, you proved it on these holidays. All the money in the world couldn't have saved these people. But you did; you won over the villagers. You read the books. Our little paradise by the sea would be nothing without you."

He leaned in, closer. "I would be nothing without you."

This close, I could feel the heat of Booker's body, I could smell the manly scent of his cologne. I reached up, tentatively, to run my fingers through his hair. I couldn't understand how someone could feel this way about little old me. But I was beginning to learn that some things, you just didn't question. *I kissed him.*

Our lips locked, and we stood, delighting in the feel of each other's lips on a beach that was all ours, for so long that I was breathless when we parted. "I feel faint," I giggled. "I haven't had a kiss like that in a long time!"

Booker reached down, and then his arms were around my back and he was scooping me into the air. "In that case, maybe we'd better find you somewhere to lie down!"

I squealed, before clapping my hands over my mouth. "Booker!" I whispered. "What are you doing!" I knew exactly what he intended. And there was no way I was having any of it on a beach out in the open.

He grinned, like he had read my mind, walking me up the beach to put me down at the sands edge. My back pressed into a palm tree as he kissed me again. One hand went to my hips, caressing my curves. The other to his own shirt, unbuttoning slowly.

"Booker! What if someone sees?"

"That again?" he asked, shirt slipping off his shoulders. They were bronzed from the tropical sun, rippling smoothly as they worked. The shirt fell to the ground.

He was a masterpiece—if I saw him like this every day, I would never grow tired. "What if I get dirty?" The protests were getting less and less convincing, even to me.

He grinned, then looked to the shirt. "That's what that's for. Not that we're going to need it yet."

I raised an eyebrow, hands running over his bulging chest. A masterpiece indeed. "And why not?"

He reached down to pluck a long strand of grass from the tufts that grew between sand and forest. He ran it up my arm, goosebumps trailing quickly behind it. I was in a simple strapless summer dress over a bikini. I would never have been brave enough to wear it back home, but here…

He grasped the dress with one hand and pulled it gently down, exposing the bikini. "Because I want to tease you first, that's why." The grass drifted down over my bosom, tickling the skin wherever it touched with a caress that was almost maddening. It hit my bikini top and glided over that too, pausing where it covered my nipples to circle gently. They hardened instantly; firm nubs under fabric that expressed so much better than words what this man was doing to me.

"Book-"

He cut me off with a kiss, and then his mouth drifted lower, down my neck and over my bikini. His mouth kissed the raised material in its center, then wet it and pulled back, blowing gently. Shivers ran through my whole body and I groaned. I could feel the heat starting to pool between my hips, my body responding to his touch in the only way it knew how.

I couldn't take it. I had to have him. I reached desperately for his belt, but his hands slapped me away playfully. "Not yet, my love. All in due time. I haven't thanked you yet."

"For what-"

I cut off again as Booker's other hand moved between my legs, pushing my bikini bottom to one side. A long finger entered me in that most intimate of places, and I groaned.

"You believed in me. You saved this island."

I could feel his finger sliding inside, my body already wet from his touch.

His hard body pushed against mine, chest flattening my breasts against me. "But enough words." His finger began to move slowly in and out and my legs almost buckled. My head leaned back against the palm tree as I sucked in a deep breath.

What was he doing to me? How could he command my every thought with just one little finger? Another slid inside to join the first and I moaned, enjoying the stretching sensation—the curl of his fingers as they caressed my wall, the titillation of each knuckle as they glided in and out. Those little sparks that he'd first introduced me to were back, running up my spine and down my legs—the waves lapping at the shore, and the bright stars overhead serving only to intensify the experience. There was something about being outdoors— about the chance of being discovered—that electrified.

I felt Booker kiss my neck once more, and then his mouth was sucking warmly on a nipple, lavishing it with attention as his fingers moved in constant rhythm below. The mouth changed to the other breast, and suddenly one nipple was warm and the other cold; wet in the cool night air. The sensation was delightful, and now the sparks were shivers inside me that matched those that had sprung across my breasts.

"Booker. Make love to me."

His mouth lifted from my body. "I intend to. But not quite yet." He kissed my nipple again, and then started to slide lower. I could feel his descent traced in shivers that moved with his mouth; down the underside of my breasts, across my hips and then to that place between my legs where his fingers still worked. He pushed my legs apart, and I complied, feeling the electricity building and leaning back against the smooth trunk of the palm to give his mouth access.

Then I felt his warm breath on that most private of places. And his lips began to suckle me just as they had my nipples.

His warm mouth upon my body. His fingers possessing me just below. *The shivers inside were building faster than I'd ever thought possible.*

I could feel his tongue. His fingers. And they were both picking up pace. The shivers were in every part of my body. I couldn't hold on anymore—not like this. His mouth had barely touched me, but I was going to… I was going to…

"Son of a Biscuit!"

I threw my head back and vocalized my pleasure to the night sky, not caring how far the scream travelled as my body began to convulse around Booker's fingers and mouth. When I was done, he came up grinning. I seized him, eyes wild. "What have you done to me? How did that happen so fast?"

He reached for his belt, stepping out of his clothing to stand naked in the sand. "Don't worry, the next one will be slower."

He pulled me toward the water, and we lay down just above it, the fabric of his spread shirt a makeshift blanket on the dry sand beneath us. If I stretched my toes I might touch the water, but I wasn't thinking about that. Not now. Not with this gorgeous man above me. Every bit of him was perfect—from tanned shoulders, to the ripple of muscles that ran down his stomach, and the hair just below. My hand reached down and grasped him, enjoying his size within my palm. *Perfect indeed.*

We lay there, like a scene from Casablanca, kissing on the beach side by side. My hand slid up and down, admiring how hard he was. Yes. This was what I wanted. I rolled onto my back and he moved above me.

He slid in with a smooth motion that was all pleasure, reminding me of how easily he had delighted my body but moments ago. Our mouths locked. And then he began to move gently; in time to the sound of the waves. I could feel him all the way inside, deeper than his fingers, and different—better perhaps, in the way that I knew him more intimately now, in the way that this brought us both pleasure.

We moved together with no rush, enjoying the night and each other, letting sensation build slowly. But soon the waves weren't moving fast enough, and our bodies began to quicken. Now they were moving in time with our breathing, and the waves were inside me—washing electric pleasure through my body in ripples that spread in circles from between my legs.

Elbows in the sand, all I could do was move my hips, kissing him as he kissed me, encouraging him with looks in my eyes as he moved faster on my body. He was in control now, though we both rocked in time, the night air on my skin cooling the heat our actions were generating.

The pleasure was starting to spike—the waves inside me now rising higher and higher with each thrust of his hips, as if his motions were whipping up a storm, or perhaps the earth was moving along lines of pleasure that were throwing the oceans into turmoil.

Suddenly my fists clenched. Not again, surely? Not so soon. And suddenly it wasn't a matter of if I would make it; it was a matter of holding off as long as possible. His long, hard member thrilled with every thrust.

I tried to think of something, anything to dull the waves washing through me, but my mind was blank. I was a rowboat in a hurricane, and the storm in my body must soon capsize all logical thought. I began to groan.

Booker, the traitor, simply grinned and began to move faster.

Then I noticed the look in his eyes—a wild look that said he understood my pleasure. That his own mirrored it. And I knew that if I was going to sink beneath the waves, it would be taking him down with me.

I began thrusting back onto him, doubling his movements; his breathing growing ragged in response. One hand lifted from the sand to grasp his neck, supporting myself on him, riding him hard and fast until both our eyes were glazed. I felt his final swell within me just as the foaming waves of pleasure finally crashed upon the shore of my own soul. We both threw back our heads and cried our delight, our bodies continuing to move until that sweet ache of release had coursed through me. Time seemed to skip a beat, and we were suddenly panting, lying back in the sand, replete.

"One more night before reality kicks back in," I struggled when I could talk. I rolled on top of him, reaching down for his still hard member. "Might as well make the most of it then, right?"

PART 4:

BY THE WAY

When Clara stands up to the nasty wife of her handsome Billionaire lover, the stakes quickly rise. His wife would do anything to get her hands on Booker's money. Even kill…

Will Clara and Booker survive to live happily ever after? The story concludes in *By the Way*.

PROLOGUE

Urgh. Monday morning blues had never been this bad.
But then, my weekend had never been spent on my own
private tropical island before, either—it was always going
to be rough.

Showing photos to Sandra while it snowed outside
almost made up for it: Booker standing bare chested in the
sand, the village kids playing, the cave art that had become
the island's saving grace. Each one brought an *ooh* from
Sandra, but meant so much more to me.

Already I longed to go back.

I sighed. *We'd better start saving.*

Booker was signing the divorce papers today. With
them, he was signing a document handing over everything
he owned to his wife. I didn't know exactly how much that
was, but it had to be a lot—probably millions, considering
the boat and island.

I didn't care about Booker's money, not really. But I
did care about dating a married man. Or at least, I'd
thought I did. Now I wasn't so sure—that pre-nup just
made me angry: *Should either party engage in relations of a sexual*

nature with a person outside of the marriage, that person will forfeit all wealth, including land, stock, and cash reserves, to the other party; on the proviso that concrete evidence can be presented in a court of law incriminating either the cheating partner or their mistress.

I'd shrugged, the first time I'd heard it. Booker and I were together, but his wife had a new man too—shouldn't that cancel each other out?

"Listen to that last line again," he'd said. "*Either the cheating partner, or their mistress.* It only counts if you cheat with a woman."

One little line. One crazy, tiny little interpretation that had changed the entire meaning of the contract. I hated Booker's wife for holding him to it. I hated her for many things truthfully—how she treated Booker, how she took delight in hunting endangered animals.

Booker strode into the library, distracting me from my thoughts.

"Did you sign it?" I asked, tentatively.

"On my way there now. Thought I'd pop in for a little moral support before I did."

I guess this must be a big day for him. "You ok?"

A hand went to the back of his neck. "Yes, I'll be fine." He forced a smile. "It's just... $4.3 billion is a lot to lose in a single day."

Behind me, books fell to the floor as Sandra gasped in shock. My own face went white. I'd known he was wealthy, but... "Did you just say *billion*?"

He nodded. "Not all cash, obviously. But that's the value of the assets."

"Booker—I never knew!"

He shrugged. "I didn't think it mattered, not really. It will be zero by the end of the day."

I shook my head. The thought of his horrible wife getting that much made me feel physically sick.

"Booker." My voice came out in a whisper. "Don't go."

The man laughed, mistaking my intentions. "I'd like to stay all day too, but you've got work and I've got a divorce paper to sign."

"No, that's not what I mean."

He cocked his head, not quite sure where I was going.

Where was I going? There'd been something on my mind for a while now. Something at the back of my head that had started on the island, when I'd learned that sometimes you just needed to trust someone. I'd been thinking a lot about the power of words, and their interpretation too.

It might be silly but… "Booker, if you had to define the word sexual, how would you do it?"

He looked to me. "Using as few words as possible?"

I nodded.

He grinned. "You."

I punched him in the arm. "That's not what I mean, and you know it."

"What do you mean then?"

"Well, I guess I was thinking about the terms of that pre-nuptial agreement. I've been thinking about it all morning. It says 'should you engage in relations of a sexual nature,' right?"

Booker nodded.

"Well, what exactly does 'sexual' mean?"

His hand went to his chin. "That's a pretty hard one to define—sex, I guess? Though Clinton got caught out with that one."

"But a sexual act of some sort, right? It can't just mean 'holding hands.'"

Booker looked at me. "Where are you going with this?"

"Well, I was just thinking. If we don't admit that we're having sex, and provided we don't actually do it in public, how are they ever going to prove that clause in your contract?"

Booker looked thoughtful. "I guess I just always thought that the two went hand in hand. If you're dating someone… you have sex with them."

He held up his hand, realization dawning in his eyes. "But of course, that's not true at all, is it? I mean, I've got friends myself that are waiting until marriage."

"So…" I voiced what was on my mind. "Why do you have to give over your money?"

Booker's hand went to the back of his head. "Because my wife knows about you now. She'll never agree to a divorce without it." He moved toward me. "And I know how you feel about being with a married man."

I walked several paces away then turned to him, hands out. *Here it came.* The words I thought I'd never utter. "So… what if I told you that I think I might be okay with that?"

Booker looked at me. "With what?"

"With you being married. I'm starting to learn that love doesn't always follow the rules. So maybe I shouldn't either." I moved toward him again. "Booker. Don't divorce her. I know you've said you'd give it all up. But you shouldn't have to."

He shook his head. "That's very sweet of you, but you're forgetting one little problem."

I slumped. "What's that?"

"My wife's a bitch. She'd haul both of us before the courts and make us testify under oath that we didn't love each other." His hands went to my shoulders, and he looked deep into my eyes. "I couldn't do that. Ever."

I kissed him, then pulled away. I wasn't ready to give up. Not just yet. "Now you're the one being sweet. But I think you're forgetting one little thing yourself."

An eyebrow rose. "Oh, and what's that?"

"Until that contract is signed, you're the one with all the money. How long do you think your lawyers could delay things for, if they tried? Months? Years?"

Booker grew thoughtful. "My wife does have money— many of our accounts were shared. But it's true, I have the businesses, therefore I've got a hell of a lot more. It could work." He looked to me. "But it would mean hiding… this. What we have."

I shook my head. "Not at all. We could be seen in public, we could hold hands, heck we could officially be an item. As long as we don't have sex in front of a video camera, we're not in a sexual relationship."

"What about kissing? Is that considered sexual?"

I paused. "I don't know. I guess we could ask the lawyers. But if Bill Clinton got away with arguing that a blow job wasn't 'sexual relations,' I suspect we're safe."

His arms folded around me. "Would you do that? For me?"

I nodded. "And to pay back your wife. I've never met her and I know she's a bitch. Let's drag this out as long as we can—who knows, she might even just get sick of the whole thing and go away!"

Booker chuckled. "You definitely haven't met my wife if you think that. But you're right. Why give her everything that she wants on a silver platter? Even if it means one more holiday together, I think it's worth it."

"Just promise me one thing," I said, snuggling into his chest.

"Anything."

"No more holidays where the secret plan is to blow things up, ok?"

He burst out laughing. "Deal!" Then he swept me into his arms, dipping me almost to the floor like a damsel from an old-time movie. He kissed me, before swinging me back up. "Let's do something tonight. To celebrate!"

"Pizza?"

He shook his head. "I have something a bit more special in mind. I'll pick you up at sunset."

CHAPTER ONE

My first hint about our destination tonight was the package waiting for me on my doorstep: a white box with black edging and six letters printed across it—*Chanel*. I looked wildly left and right when I saw it, first disbelieving that the box was on *my* actual doorstep, and then disbelieving that it hadn't already been stolen.

I opened it as soon as I was through the door, eyes going wide at the cocktail dress that slid through my fingers from within. Dress me up and call me Sally—it was beautiful!

It felt smooth against my body—knee length, with a cute flared skirt and a layered top. The gossamer outer revealed perhaps just a little more cleavage than I was normally comfortable with, but *son of a biscuit* I'd look hot! Black Chanel heels lay under it. I pulled them out—I'd never even owned Chanel perfume, now I felt like I was modelling for them!

My second hint about where we were going was when, just as the light began to fade, I looked over the balcony to see a cherry red Ferrari pull up out the front. I ran down the stairs as fast as I was able to in my new heels.

"You look beautiful!" Booker exclaimed when he saw me. Then he whistled. "Remind me to take you out more often."

"It looks ok?" I asked, patting my hair. "Since you won't tell me where we're going, I kind of had to just do something to match the dress."

He shook his head. "You did well, Sheets. It's perfect."

"Will I need a coat?"

He shook his head, taking my arm. "There's a jacket in the trunk if you need it, but it should be quite warm where we're going."

We walked outside, my shoes crunching across thin snow. Despite the cool weather I wasn't cold—perhaps something do to with the hot man beside me. "So are you going to tell me, or keep me guessing?"

He shrugged. "It's a cocktail party, but I think you'll like it. Only happens for three weeks a year, and you have to know someone important to get in." His hand pulled two golden tickets from his pocket, and he grinned at me. "It just so happens, I know important people."

* * *

Even when I was younger, I'd never been a car girl—a teeny-bopper-speed-racer that fancied herself in a black and white checked bikini. I hadn't been the type to *ooh* and *aah* over every V6 that drove by.

But I knew what a Ferrari was. And I knew as soon as I sank into its impossibly low seats that I was in trouble.

My hands ran over the leather of my seat in awe. There was something… *primal*, about sitting in an Italian supercar. Not the leather, though that felt so soft I could be stroking a small animal. Or the smell—which was all new money and old school power. Or even the engine, which purred through my senses like a one ton cat.

It was the fantasy. It was that sleek red shape and deep bass throb that woke something at the back synapses. Just sitting in a Ferrari made you feel sexier.

For the first time in my life I knew what all those girls on street corners felt like—because all I could think about was jumping the driver too.

We motored out of the city and into the darkening countryside.

I had to do it, it was just too hot a car not to. "How long till we get there?"

"About 15 minutes, it's a little out of town."

Long enough. Continuing to face forward, my hand closest to him crept into his lap.

Booker started. "What are you doing?"

"You just keep your eyes on the road," I said. "We don't want any accidents now."

By touch alone I found the zipper of his pants. I inched it down, pulling free the quickly hardening bulk below it. For once, I'd taken him by surprise, and I enjoyed the sensation of him growing firmer as I held him. It was like those videos of trees growing by time delay—the trunk pushing ever higher, growing thicker every second.

A car flashed past unknowing, and I stole a glace. His member was standing at glorious hardness behind the steering wheel, rising tall and erect from his clothes. And I'd done nothing except hold him! The thought sent a thrill through me. *Just wait until I really got started!*

I began to stroke slowly, careful not to move my shoulder—the Ferrari was getting enough attention already as it zoomed down the road; we didn't want to give anyone a reason to look closer. Booker let out a murmur of appreciation, one hand reaching blindly for my breasts as he drove. I paused to slap it away. "Bad boy, you'll ruin the dress."

His hand went back to the steering wheel reluctantly.

"You just keep your eyes on the road."

I continued to work him slowly, looking straight ahead, as if we were both out for an evening drive and my hand wasn't wrapped around his *gear stick*.

But it was. I could feel his soft, velvety skin as my hand moved up and down. A smooth shaft that rose high in the air. The head, with its supersensitive skin. His breathing started to get heavier as my strokes took effect.

My breathing was getting heavier too.

My seatbelt unclicked as it got darker and the roads quieter, and I swiveled in my seat to face him. Booker glanced at me briefly, the car swerving slightly, and I bit my lip. This was fun! I swapped him to my other hand, then leaned into him to kiss his neck. The car jerked forward, Booker's foot pushing reflexively down on the pedal before bringing it back under control.

Ahead, the white headlights of his Ferrari lit a winding country road; white snow piled high on either side of the car. The bare branches of trees curved in and out of sight, heavy with snow, as he drove, and I stroked. *Where were we going?*

I looked down at him, and suddenly decided I didn't care—I was having fun right here, anything else was a bonus. My hand began to twist on his shaft; turning in one direction as it rose, then in the other as it came back down.

Booker's breaths were a pant. His hand slid into my lap, pushing under my skirt briefly to feel the heat between my legs. "What say we stop this car?"

I shook my head, returning his hand to the wheel. "You'll ruin the dress. Why don't we leave that for our way home?" My hand continued to rise up and down. I nuzzled his neck again. "And it will be fun, I promise. We can go to a lookout like we're teenagers again. I can straddle your lap, and then…"

I began to stroke faster. Booker groaned.

A bead of moisture appeared at his tip. I wiped it away with my thumb, sending shivers through him, then added the motion to my actions; my thumb rolling over the top of him each time I crested his tip. *Twist and then roll. Twist and then roll.* Booker's breathing was soon strained, his eyes fixed desperately on the road.

I could tell he was getting close.

"Does the seat go back in this thing?" Before Booker could answer I had found the lever, and then my seat was as far back as it could go.

I lowered myself to my knees in the leg space I had created, facing him across the center console.

"What are you doing *now*?" he asked.

My head lowered into his lap. "What do you think I'm about to do?"

I brushed a strand of hair behind my ear and didn't wait for a response; my mouth sliding down over his shaft to wet it. When I came back up, his knuckles were white on the steering wheel. I leaned up to kiss him on the cheek—he acted tough, but sometimes he was so cute!— then returned to begin bobbing up and down in earnest.

The car picked up speed, a mirror for his arousal, a deep throb climbing from the floor into my whole body. It felt good, and I considered actually telling Booker to stop the car before deciding against it. We had somewhere to be, and I just knew I'd rip the dress—better to wait till the ride home.

My tongue resumed its rolling, lapping up his shaft to caress his tip; curling around his head before sinking my whole mouth down on him. Up, down, up, down. I felt Booker's hand rest briefly on my head, a gesture of encouragement, and I began to move faster, sucking myself down; gripping the base of his shaft as I pulled my lips back up.

"Babe. We're two minutes away; you'd better come back up." Booker's voice was strained, a herculean effort of concentration.

Two minutes hey? Let's see what I could do in two minutes.

My mouth moved even faster, hands now sliding up and down as well.

"Clara, we're almost there," Booker said urgently, panic rising. "What are you doing? Come up!"

I giggled. "Making sure you go from *almost there* to *there*."

He groaned in pleasure as I gave him a hard suck.

"Oh god—I think you're going to do it, too!"

My fist was slipping up and down in a flurry now, my head hovering at the tip to lick the moisture beading away from him. I sensed us turning off the main road as Booker groaned. The engine revved as his foot misjudged the peddle. *Almost there.*

My lips lowered back over him. I sucked, hard, and slid as far down as I could. His hand went to the back of my head and I felt him suddenly swell at the back of my throat. *Yes!*

I came back up just as he released with a cry, my lips remaining around his head to collect his hot load on my tongue. I swallowed as the engine began to slow and then rose quickly, hand dabbing delicately at my lips.

My goodness, we really were almost there!

The car stopped just moments later. Booker adjusted himself, and then a valet was opening the door.

CHAPTER TWO

"You know, for two people that have just decided that the only way to keep *several billion* dollars is not to get caught having sexual relations in public, we just walked a very fine line."

I grinned, hand going to my lips again at the memory. The valet had just driven away. "I know. But it was crazy good fun, wasn't it?"

Booker shook his head. "I'm pretty sure we're going to get caught eventually. But it'll be one hell of a ride until then." He took my arm. "Shall we?"

A red carpet snaked through the snow before us. Flickering lamps placed at measured intervals led to a warehouse just beyond.

"Where are we?"

Booker just smiled, then led me down the carpet until we were standing before large metal doors. The warehouse was an old corrugated iron affair, several stories high, with all the windows boarded up. Like an abandoned aircraft hangar, but with a flat roof instead of curved. We'd driven all the way into the countryside to go to a warehouse?

I noticed a butler standing in bowtie and tails to one side.

"The whole thing looks kind of shabby, doesn't it?" Booker said, leading us to the butler. He was enjoying the look of confusion on my face.

"Umm…"

"Just wait till you see inside." Booker handed over two golden tickets.

The butler inspected them, then snapped his heels together. "Very good, sir." He pressed a discrete button on the wall behind him, and the huge double doors swung inward.

Well roll me up and call me curly.

I stood, mouth open, on the threshold of another world; an exotic fantasy land that was half harem, half Turkish bazaar. Stretching into the distance was a vast space, carpeted in rich red Turkish rugs and a million silk cushions. Drapes covered the walls, and silk canopied across the ceiling; held in place by exotic glass lanterns that dangled, flickering, on chains to cast an intimate light.

Beneath, scattered braziers burned with a cheerful glow. Women in veiled dresses walked among them serving heaped plates of exotic delicacies. There were several hundred well-dressed guests inside; bare chested men in Aladdin pants were offering them trays of steaming Turkish tea and mysterious cocktails. I looked to Booker.

He winked at me. "Staying rich does have its perks. You get to go to the most awesome parties."

It was like we'd somehow stumbled into a scene from *Arabian Nights.*

Along with *Pride and Prejudice*—and now the *Karma Sutra*—the book was one of my favorite romances. I loved the theme—of Scheherazade, a beautiful woman sentenced to death by an Arabian king, but who every night told such exciting tales that each morning the king spared her life for one more day.

It took 1001 nights for the king to fall in love with Scheherazade and change her life. It had only taken Booker one to change mine.

A waiter approached us and Booker took a drink. My hand hovered over steaming hot tea but chose a clear cocktail in a long stemmed glass instead. I took a sip, and discovered with delight that I was drinking something that tasted exactly like Turkish delight.

I looked up to find Booker watching me with a smile. "What?" I asked self-consciously.

His thumb went to my jawline, caressing it. "You just look so cute, that's all. It gives me so much pleasure to see you enjoying yourself."

I leaned in close, grinning cheekily. "That's funny," I said into his ear. "I was thinking the same thing about you on the car ride here."

I was rewarded with a sputter as Booker almost choked on his drink.

He flicked liquid from where it had splashed on his hand. "Come on, let's explore before I decide to throw four billion dollars out the window and take you right here and now."

* * *

I didn't know which was more amazing—the shirtless musclebound man walking around blowing spouts of flame into the air, or the camel in another corner bedecked in rich, red riding carpet, with tassels around its neck. The camel perhaps—but only because I had no idea how they'd managed to find one in the middle of little-old-here, *in the snow*.

"Booker, this is amazing." We had retired to cushions in a darkened, private corner to treat ourselves on the plentiful trays of *meze* walking regularly past us.

So far I'd had tiny shish kebobs, fried pastries, miniature peppers stuffed with feta, glazed pecans and baklava, which I'd discovered was a rich, sweet pastry made of layers of filo filled with chopped nuts and honey. I'd waved the serving girl back for a second helping of that one, my mouth still full as I motioned her to heap my plate high. I was having the most wonderful evening—I felt like a princess, with Booker my handsome prince.

"I've never been here before, but I'd heard stories," Booker said. "A place that caters to the fabulously wealthy—people fly in from all over the country to the private airport just nearby."

I couldn't believe I'd never heard of something like this. "But how does it even exist? And why on earth have you never been before?"

Booker shrugged, choosing to answer my second question first. "I guess I've never had someone to share it with," he said. "A couple of people I know have been pestering me to go for the last few years, but it's really something I wanted to do as a couple, and well…" Booker didn't need to say any more. Two years ago was around the time when things had started to go sour with his wife.

"Who just organizes a random three week extravaganza for the mega rich?" I asked, trying to distract him from the path I'd led him down.

He brightened. "Oh that's easy. The tickets more than make this worthwhile for the organizers, and it's a great place to network with your peers. The people that do this are pretty well known in the right circles."

I looked at the extravagance surrounding us. A belly dancer had begun performing nearby, and… was that man with the oiled scalp swallowing a sword?

"How much are tickets?" I asked, eyes narrowed.

"Nice try, but my lips are sealed." He shook his head. "You don't need to know."

A sudden suspicion occurred to me, and I looked down at my Chanel dress. "More or less than this dress?"

He raised an eyebrow, but shook his head once more.

"The dress and the shoes combined?"

He laughed, shaking his head again. "I'm not telling. But it was worth it, if you're enjoying yourself."

"You drive a Ferrari and own a boat bigger than a cruise liner. 'It was worth it' tells me nothing!"

* * *

I'd been having the most wonderful, extravagant, amazing time. But that all came to a crashing halt when I visited the Ladies' Room.

It wasn't the surrounds; just like everything else here, they were beautiful—Italian marble walls with waterfall basins, rolled soft towelettes; an assortment of expensive perfumes for those that wanted a refresh.

Rather, it was who was waiting for me when I exited my stall. He was tall with a ratty face, and I recognized him immediately, despite the fact that he'd swapped trench coat for tuxedo.

"Simon Wickson, Private Investigator," I said, a sour taste suddenly in my mouth. I looked around and noted that the rest of the bathroom was empty. "How did you get in here?"

"Clara! What a lovely surprise. How are you?"

"Fine, thank you," I said curtly. "But you'll have to excuse me, I have somewhere to be." I brushed past him to wash my hands.

"So my client, *Mrs. Devale*, told me something very interesting today."

"Oh yes, and what's that?" I asked, soaping my hands quickly. I couldn't wait to get out—my hands might be getting cleaner, but I was feeling dirtier every minute spent talking to him.

"*Mr. DeVale* never showed up for his appointment today."

"Well that's her business, not mine." I dried myself and pushed past him toward the door.

His hand went to my shoulder, stopping me firmly. "But I think it is your business. *You never came good on our deal,* Clara."

"Sell out Booker? I'm sorry, but that wasn't much of a deal." I pried his fingers from my shoulder. "Excuse me, I no longer want to talk to you."

"Ah, but I need to talk to you. You see, Clara, I don't think you realize the situation you're in right now."

I stopped. "And what's that?" I said, rounding on him. "That Booker's wife isn't going to get her dirty mitts on his hard-won money?"

He nodded. "Exactly. My client is a very passionate woman. *She hunts animals for sport. She wields power like a baseball bat.* How do you think getting all that taken away would make her feel?"

"I don't care how she feels," I retorted.

"Ah, but you should. Because having her unhappy is a very serious problem for you."

A shiver went down my spine. "Are you threatening me?"

"Of course not. I'm just saying that you really should consider your options before you—or Booker—get hurt."

"You can't threaten me. That's blackmail."

He shook his head. "I told you, I'm not threatening you. Nobody wants to go to jail here."

He grinned, an insincere show of yellow teeth. "Did you know that if Mr. DeVale dies, his entire fortune goes to his loving wife?"

"She wouldn't!"

"Wouldn't what? I'm not implying anything. Although I do understand your confusion—$4.3 billion is a lot of money. I'm sure there are people who would kill to keep something like that. Not that I know any of course."

"Get out," I said, finger trembling as I pointed at the door.

He smiled, and moved toward the exit. "Do enjoy the party, Clara. I'm sorry I can't stay. I've got some arrangements I need to be making."

He rested a calling card on the benchtop beside the door. "The arrangements won't be ready until Friday—perhaps we can speak again before then? Mrs. DeVale is *so* eager to complete negotiations."

CHAPTER THREE

I was still shaken the following day. I'd been having such a wonderful night, and then in one foul swoop that had all been ruined. We'd gone home immediately after; me ashen faced, Booker puzzled at my sudden quietness. But I couldn't tell him about this. Not yet. Not until I knew how I felt about it myself.

That investigator had threatened to hurt me. Even worse, he'd threatened harm to Booker. Not that he'd been stupid enough to say it outright, or I'd been smart enough to record him doing it.

Perhaps… perhaps I should consider signing that document? Booker had been happy to lose the money before. And I'd been happy to too, until I'd realized how much was at stake. Was I just being greedy? Did I value money more than I did Booker's life?

I shook my head. The money was just the most visible part of the equation. It was what his wife would do with it that really mattered—more than just make us poor, or miserable.

With absolutely nothing, we'd be helpless against her. That island—the one we'd protected? I suddenly wondered how even World Heritage listing could stand against $4.3 billion in pressure. The woman would be unstoppable.

The thought made me depressed, so I did the thing I usually did when I was down. I walked to my bookshelf and picked up a book.

I considered my copy of *The Karmasutra* first. But it reminded me too much of Booker. He'd personalized the edition himself, and as I flicked through the pages morosely all I could think of was that soon, perhaps this might be the only piece of him left.

The book went back on the shelf and my hand drifted further along the spines. *Pride and Prejudice*… no. *Saltwater Kisses*… no, *Casanova*…

I picked the book up. I'd always loved *Casanova*, even before Booker had stood under my balcony with a string quartet behind him and quoted verse from it. The namesake of the story was a rascal, a rogue with an insatiable appetite for women and adventure. *A charlatan, a gambler and a liar, too.* But if you could look past all that, the story of his long and complicated romance with a woman known only as M.M. was fascinating reading.

I flicked to my favorite part idly, where Casanova described an encounter he'd had with her after saying he had eaten a salad with six egg whites for lunch:

> *Then I picked her up, and she put her arms around my shoulders to lighten her weight. I seized her thighs and she braced herself on my nail; but after walking all around the room and fearing the worst, I put her down on the carpet. I sat down with her in my lap, and with her beautiful hand she obliged me by finishing the task, culling the first egg white in her palm. "Only to five to go," she said, cleaning her hand.*

So scandalous! The book was one part humor, one part arousal, and one part fascinating insight into the customs of the 18th century.

They'd been so much freer about their sexuality back then. It had been common for nobles to own love pads that contained erotic paintings on the walls, mirrors on the ceiling, hidden entrances and even secret rooms with spyholes where lovers could 'sit back and enjoy the show.' Casanova had made love to M.M. in one such pleasure room, owned by the Ambassador to France. And he'd done it while knowing that the Ambassador might be in the other room, watching their every move.

Once upon a time, this voyeurism had been the only part of Casanova's tale that had ever felt uncomfortable to me. But now… I thought I understood the appeal. *Making love to Booker on that beach. Pleasuring him in the car.* There was something risqué about the danger of being watched. Something that heightened the pleasure—at least occasionally, and only if you weren't caught.

Just imagine what Casanova would be up against nowadays! There'd be a video camera behind the spyhole…

The thought took me to thinking about the wire I had worn that second time Booker and I had made love. I still had it here, somewhere. I'd thought I was doing the right thing—protecting myself by recording our conversation; driving him back to his wife.

But now… I'd done just the opposite. By taking it off, I'd endangered us both.

I'd always believed that good conquered all in the end—in books, the bad guys never won. But this was real life. And it looked like the bad girl was going to win.

Casanova had been jailed once for witchcraft. But if Booker died, there was no magic witches' brew that could bring him back. There was no secret enchantment or elixir of life I'd be able to feed him. He'd just be dead, and my stupid inability to protect Booker would have cost me any chance I ever had of happiness.

I flicked to the section of the book where Casanova had escaped imprisonment. There had to be something that I could do to escape this too. *Something that would protect us from Booker's wife.*

But she had an ironclad agreement that would give her Booker's money. And there was nothing, as far as I could see, that she valued more than that.

> *I admit that I am proud of my escape; but my pride does not come from having succeeded… it comes from my having concluded that the thing could be done and having had the courage to undertake it.*

There was, I realized, something I could do. Something that I'd known all along, really. Something the private investigator had told me about the very first time I'd met him. In fact, he'd been telling me repeatedly. I'd just been refusing to listen.

… it comes from my having concluded that the thing could be done and having had the courage to undertake it. Did I have the courage to do it? Was I really prepared to risk everything for Booker, just like he'd been willing to for me?

Yes. Yes I was. I snapped the book shut and pulled a small white calling card from my pocket. The phone picked up immediately when I rang.

"I'll do it," I said, taking a deep breath. "But I want to look her in the face when I do. I want to meet the wife in person."

CHAPTER FOUR

The café out front of the library was officially closed at this time of night, but knowing the owners afforded certain advantages—and dropping Booker's name afforded even more. It was important that Booker's wife and I meet alone, where we could both feel safe saying what needed to be said. The café had seemed the perfect place for that to happen.

What I hadn't counted on, was that sitting waiting for a woman with the power to ruin my life would also make me smile. Potted trees graced the floor of the cafe, ferns and vines hung from roof and walls, and there, with books for legs and a timber top, was the picnic table upon which Booker and I had made love.

I sat down at it, grinning, and ran my fingers across the polished grain. It seemed appropriate to be here, somehow.

I heard the door open a short while later. I smoothed down my dress and sat a little straighter. *Showtime.*

"So we meet at last." Booker's wife stood framed in the doorway, a practiced pose I'm sure she'd modelled in the mirror before arriving.

She was slightly older than I'd imagined, with long blonde hair and full red lips. Tight jeans, designer top and—I had to bite my lip—the fur of something black and grey hanging lifeless around her neck.

I stood up, determined to be polite. "Hello, I'm Clara."

She strode in, ignoring my outstretched hand. "Clara." She made the name sound like a punch to the stomach. "So you're the woman who's fucking my husband."

I wiped my hand on my top as if I hadn't just been snubbed. "Um… Well I guess I should apologize for that. I never-"

"Look, let's just cut the bullshit, shall we?" Her words cut across me like a bulldozer. "I fly to Paris in an hour." Her long legs click-clacked to a nearby table and she ran a finger across its top disapprovingly. "I don't give a rat's ass whether you're fucking him or sucking him—as long as his balls have touched your body in some manner or other, I'm happy."

"Well-"

She pulled a crisp sheet of monogrammed paper from a deep snakeskin purse at her side. "Just put your signature here, and we'll get this over and done with."

I hesitated, eyes avoiding her. "Actually, I was hoping we could settle this amicably."

There was silence. I looked up.

Her eyes were narrowed. "This *is* being amicable."

"I… well, I was kind of hoping we could talk about the conditions of the pre-nuptial arrangement. You know, woman to woman."

Her eyes narrowed even further, a viper paused before the strike. "What about it?"

"Well, it's really a technicality, isn't it? You're with someone, he's with someone-"

"So?"

"So it was obviously a typo, the word 'mistress', right? If I signed this, would you agree to sharing the money? Splitting it 50:50?"

"I don't share well."

"Well maybe," I said, getting fed up, "I won't share my signature!"

The woman suddenly smiled, like we were best friends on a girl's day out, and indicated the pelt around her neck. "Do you like it?" she asked, giving a little turn. "Clouded leopard cub—they've got the softest fur."

The sudden change took me by surprise. "That's… um, no. Sorry, but actually I don't."

The smile left her face like it had never been there. She stalked toward me. "*Good.* You're not meant to like it. You're meant to be reminded when you see it of the power I have. I can do anything I want. *Kill* anything I want."

I backed away. "Are… are you threatening me?"

"Just sign the form."

"And if I don't?"

"You don't want to go there."

I put the pen on a nearby table, continuing to back away. "This was a mistake. I don't like you. And I don't want you to get Booker's money. You're already with someone else, why can't you just be happy for him too?"

She began stalking toward me. "Because he has things I want. And I told you, I don't share well."

"You're a horrible person, you know that?"

I'd backed up as far as I could go. Her finger jabbed into my breast. "Sign the form."

I shook my head. "No, I've changed my mind."

"Sign the form."

"No!"

Her eyes narrowed, and then suddenly she was so close I could see the mascara smudges under her eyes. "God dammit you little cunt! Sign the form or I'll fucking slit your throat and wear your skin like this leopard!"

I wanted to melt into the wall. My body started to shake. "You can't talk to me like that."

"I can talk to you any way I want. I'll fucking kill you, I swear it!" Spittle was frothing at her lips. "I'll chop off your fingers one by one, until there's just two left. *Then* I'll make you sign the form and shove the last two down your throat so far you'll think its Booker's dick! I can make you disappear just like that." She clicked her fingers. "There wouldn't be enough left of you to piss on when I'm done."

I'd never had anyone speak to me like that, ever. I stared at her, a hare in headlights.

"You don't think I could do it?" she snarled. "I've hunted endangered species on three continents. I slit their throats and watched them bleed out in front of me, and you know what? Nobody could do a goddamn fucking thing about it; because I was so fucking wealthy I could buy, shoot or scare anyone that stood in my way."

She looked me dead in the eyes. "I'm not losing that power. I'd kill to protect it."

She seemed to take stock of herself, calming down. "Of course, we can do it the easy way, if you want. You sign the form, I hand over the divorce papers right here and now, and we both go on our merry little way. You get what you want, I get what I want. Everyone's happy."

My shoulders slumped. "You're a nasty piece of work, you know that?"

"I know." She thrust the document into my chest. "Now sign the fucking form, before I really lose my temper."

Hand trembling, I took the affidavit. It was short, just three quick paragraphs.

> I (insert name here) attest before God and Country, upon threat of perjury and with absolute truth, that Booker DeVale and I have an ongoing sexual relationship and have knowingly been in such since (insert date here) whilst he is married to his lawful wife Stacey DeVale.

I acknowledge that my admittance of such may be used in a court of law as evidence of his infidelity, and also proof of the fact that he has cheated on his lawful wife, and that I am his mistress.

I irrevocably waive my right to council on this matter. I sign this document under my own free will.

There were tears in my eyes as my hand scrawled my name across the page.

Stacey moved to snatch it from me, but I held the shaking document up. "Your end of the bargain, please."

She pulled a sheaf of papers in a manila envelope from her bag and threw them on a nearby table. "Here. They're already signed and dated."

Then she ripped the paper from my hands and with a laugh, click clacked across the café floor, carrying Booker's entire fortune on one little piece of paper with her.

CHAPTER FIVE

Booker found me in tears shortly after; when he rang to give me goodnight words and heard me sobbing instead. He was 20 minutes away but arrived at the café within 10, the tires on his Ferrari smoking as they slid into the parking lot.

"Clara! Talk to me, what's wrong?"

I shook my head, unable to talk.

"Is it something I've done? Has someone hurt you?"

I shook my head again, head buried in his chest. "It was your wife."

"What about her? Did she do something to you?"

I wiped my eyes with my sleeve, pulling myself off Booker's chest to look him in the eyes. "She's not very nice, Booker." Even now, her crude words made me feel physically sick.

His jaw tightened. "Tell me something I don't know."

"Booker, the other night at the party…"

"Yes?"

"Her private investigator found me. He threatened me."

The confusion in his eyes began to clear. "That's why you wanted to leave early!"

I nodded.

"What did he say?" he growled.

"That if I knew what was good for me, I'd sign a form. That your wife would hurt you if I didn't."

Booker's fists clenched, and he turned, as if looking to punch something. "That bitch!"

But he didn't hit anything. Instead he turned back to me and took my shoulders. "Clara, it's okay, I'll protect you. You don't have to cry."

I sniffed again, and then snorted out a pathetic laugh. "That's not why I'm crying."

His hand went to the back of his neck. "Then why, Clara? Tell me, and I'll fix it."

"I… I met your wife."

Booker's face paled so suddenly you'd swear someone had slashed an artery. "You what? When?"

"Just now, at the café." I was on the verge of tears again. "She… she wanted me to sign a document saying we were in a sexual relationship." Now I did burst into tears, burying my face into his chest. "She said she would kill me if I didn't sign them!"

"That bitch!" Booker growled again. "Not if I don't kill her first." I'd never seen Booker so angry! "Did you do it?" he asked. "Did you sign the documents?"

I nodded into his chest.

Booker sighed. "Good, I guess. It's not how I wanted it to go, but you're more important than all the money in the world. I'm sorry you met my wife, but I'm glad you're safe."

My tears renewed. His thumb went to my cheek, wiping it dry. "It's okay, you can stop crying. It's finally over."

I shook my head, looking up at him. And for the first time, I smiled. "I don't want to stop crying."

He looked at me, confused. "What's wrong?"

"Booker," I said, laughing through my sobs. "They're tears of joy. We're finally safe."

"Well I'm glad you're taking this so well." His eyebrows rose, and he smiled too. "I guess I'm going to have to get a job! Do you think they'll have any openings at the library for me?"

I giggled, tears still streaming down my cheeks. "There's no way you'd be allowed to work at the same library as me!"

"And why not?"

"Because we'd never get any work done," I said.

I paused, pulling back off him, wiping my face. "And besides, you won't need a job."

"Why, are you going to support us both?"

I shook my head. Then I pulled a tiny black microphone from between my breasts. A cord trailed from it, down my cleavage to a USB recorder at my back. "This will."

His head cocked. "You recorded the conversation with my wife?"

I nodded. Then I unhooked the recorder and replayed it.

"I'll fucking kill you, I swear it! I'll chop off your fingers one by one, until there's just two left." His wife's voice came through the speakers, violent and cruel. *"Then I'll make you sign the form and shove the last two down your throat so far you'll think its Booker's dick! I can make you disappear just like that. There wouldn't be enough left of you to piss on when I'm done."*

Booker took the recorder from my hands. "I've heard enough," he said, face white with fury.

The smile on my face crept wider. "Really? Because I could listen to that all day."

"You're joking, right?"

"No," I said. "Do you know what this recording means?"

"Yes. My wife is a violent, homicidal maniac," he replied. "I'll be glad when I'm rid of her—even if she won."

"But she didn't."

"What?"

"Booker, she didn't win. We did."

"But she said she'd kill you, and forced you to sign the form!"

I nodded. "She did. And it was truly one of the most terrifying experiences of my life. But it was worth it Booker. *For what it means for us.*"

He nodded, thinking he understood. "I know. We may have nothing, but at least we have each other."

I shook my head. "You're still not listening. She threatened to kill me. *That's blackmail.*"

A light slowly dawned in his eyes, burning the confusion from his mind. "It is, isn't it?"

"You know what the penalty for blackmail in a court of law is, right?" I asked. *I'd looked it up.* "You go to jail for a very long time." I grinned. "What do you think her lawyer is going to say when we play this back to him?"

"I think he's going to say your signature is invalid."

"Aaand?"

"And," he said thinking, "and he would also tell her that money is worth nothing when you're in jail for 25 years. I think he'd tell her to rip up the pre-nup in the hope that we never go public with the recording."

"It's got her admitting to illegal poaching on it too," I said. I was growing excited. "We did it Booker. We found the only thing more important to her than money—her freedom. We can hold this over her head for the rest of her life!"

CHAPTER SIX

We'd called in quickly to Booker's apartment so I could reapply makeup, then driven straight back out. But this time we'd taken the Bentley, 'just for something different.'

I'd wanted to go back to the cocktail party, but Booker had shaken his head. "We've done that." Then he'd driven up a long, winding road on the outskirts of the city, bringing the Bentley to a stop at the deserted lookout at its top.

A million starry lights shone above us. A million city lights shone below. Booker reached into the back seat, and then he was popping a bottle of Cristal and pouring it into two tall champagne goblets. "To us," he said warmly.

I giggled. I'd been horrified the first time I'd done that in front of Booker. But I was doing it more and more now—something about this charming man that I was in love with had brought out the teenager within. "To us," I saluted him back. "And to your wife."

He grimaced. "Please—let's not talk about her any more. This is our night now."

I smiled coquettishly. "What do you want to talk about then?"

"I don't know—you, me… the future."

I leaned toward him, hand snaking into his lap. "How about we just chat about the first thing that comes up?"

His eyebrow rose. "Really? I thought we'd already done that."

I shook my head. "I seem to remember differently. I promised you fun on our way home, then didn't deliver. I'm thinking maybe I deliver now…"

"Right here, at the lookout?"

I nodded. "Why not? I don't want you driving, not for what I have in mind."

"But what if someone sees?"

"It doesn't matter now—that's half the fun." I poked him playfully. "What are you, chicken?"

He reached under his seat, and suddenly it was sliding all the way back. "Why don't you come here and find out."

The Bentley was a spacious car, and suddenly I was glad we were in it and not the Ferrari. I crawled into his lap, champagne forgotten.

My arms were lifted above my head, and then my dress was lying on the seat beside us. My hand went to his designer jeans. I stroked him eagerly, reaching down between my legs. "Is this our first fight?"

He shook his head. "That was some time ago, when you refused to go out with me. But this might be our third. Why don't we kiss and make up?"

"Good idea." I wiggled his jeans down and then leaned into him. Our mouths met; the feel of his hard member delightful against the cotton of my panties. I began to grind him slowly, enjoying the sensation as his hard naked shaft slid up and down me.

Booker's hands ran down the straps of my bra, caressing my covered breasts, then moved lower; over my hips and between my legs. A small jolt of electricity zapped through me when they slid behind the cotton.

It wasn't long before he had pushed the cotton aside, and we were sliding flesh on flesh. I couldn't believe how much I wanted Booker right now. How wet just the thought of a life together was making me.

I lifted myself off him, and as though we were of one mind he reached down, positioning himself below. I could feel the head of him at the lips of my opening. I lowered myself, just the tiniest bit, enjoying that initial flare and stretch of his ridge. *Then I lowered myself all the way down.*

The electricity came again, stronger this time, shimmying up my body as I slid down. That first feel of him always took my breath away. I felt like the temperature in my groin had suddenly skyrocketed. Everything started to tingle.

On top, I was in control. I began to move slowly, my hips undulating back and forth as I kept him deep in me—his member a lever which I could rock back and forth at will. He groaned, fingers raking my back, and I picked up my speed just ever so slightly. I could feel him, throbbing like a heartbeat in my core.

I closed my eyes, enjoying the sensation; the feeling of taking in all of him, the sparks as his member pushed delight through all of my body.

I wanted more of those sparks. I began to move faster, coaxing them out with every slippery movement inside me. Booker let out a groan, and I opened my eyes to find that he had closed his, lost in the pleasure of the moment. I bit my lip, anticipating his reaction, and then adjusted my legs into a squat on the seat, and began to pump up and down.

His eyes flew open as the sensation changed for the both of us, his hands moving to my backside in appreciation of the motion. "Whoa. That just bumped it up a notch."

I grinned, delighted with his reaction; delighting in my own reaction too. In this position I could feel him as deep as he'd ever been inside, reaching all the way up as if he was possessing me wholly. It was incredibly hot; I almost orgasmed just at the thought.

I'd meant to draw this out, but now? I wanted more. I wanted that pleasure to spike higher and higher, taking us both over the edge. I began to move fast upon him, bouncing up and down, the weight of my bra-bound breasts in his face as I moved. His head buried in my cleavage and then he was helping me, hands around my waist to rock me even quicker.

There was no slowing down now. Each thrust deep within drove the electricity higher. Each pull as I slid back off him was an agonizing delay to the plunge back down once more. I began to groan into his ear, head bouncing dangerously close to the roof of the car as he leaned back into the seat and we worked each other into a frenzy.

The electricity was getting halogen bright; a blinding, raging storm within me making lightning strikes with each movement. Soon the storm must break. I gritted my teeth, fighting to hold it off, fighting to prolong the pleasure. But Booker's hard thrusts and urgent breathing wouldn't allow respite—there would be no delay. He took me higher, and higher, until suddenly I was floating over the storm and I could see it breaking beneath. Lightening crackled and then I was crying my pleasure in the front seat of his car, riding his urgent thrusts as my body contracted upon him.

The hard clench of my legs was his final straw—I felt him swell and break inside me, and then he was leaning into me and pulsing a warmth which set me off all over again. Time seemed to stand still as I leaned back, the steering wheel digging into my hips, and convulsed over and over until the storm had died, and the electricity had gone from blinding lightning to warm glowing sparks.

Dimly, I became aware of a sound. I pulled off the steering wheel and it stopped. *The horn.*

I giggled as his head pulled out of my cleavage, a look of glowing pleasure on his face. "What?" he asked.

His question burst me into full bodied laughter. And I thought I was bad—he hadn't even noticed!

* * *

As Booker pulled out it left me feeling empty. *I didn't like it.* I wanted him pulsing in me forever.

He obviously had the same thought. I looked to him, he looked to me and then we were diving in the back seat like high schoolers; him ripping his jeans all the way off with an awkward hop, me quickly removing the rest of my clothing. I lay across the back seat and he climbed above me.

He was hard again already, but this time the entry was slow—a tender, delicate caress. He leaned down and kissed me. We both sighed in unison.

We made love leisurely on the back seat, taking our time; exploring each other's bodies. My hands ran over his chest and back and shoulders. I think I liked his back best, but it was a close call—his arms were deliciously thick around me, his chest defined and heavy above.

His hands explored me in turn—running over my breasts as we kissed, and then up my neck and through my hair. The feel of him inside me radiated a warm security this time. The excitement would come, but for now I was his and he was mine and if we stayed that way forever I would die happy.

Then he adjusted his angle. And the warm security faded, replaced by hot need. His motions began to grow quicker. My body moved faster in response. And suddenly the urgency was back, and his shaft was an instrument for my pleasure. I moaned, feeling the first raindrops of tension build within me; a light shower that I knew would soon become a storm.

He began to drive harder, his body moving up and down upon me. I could feel his flesh slapping into mine. Hear it as our bodies met and then withdrew, each motion stoking the storm—splashing the tension throughout my body.

My fingers dug into his back. My moans became his name, rising higher and higher as we both worked up a sweat on the fine upholstered leather.

And then he'd pulled off me, and I opened my eyes as a blast of cold air washed through the car.

"What are you doing?" I gasped.

He climbed out the door to stand naked in the snow, then pulled me toward him, still on my back. "If we're going to do it in the open, we might as well do it properly." He entered me again, leaning in close to put my legs over his shoulders and connect his tall, strong body once more.

I cried out at the unexpected pleasure of it all—the cold air on my body, the hot slap as he began to pound roughly into me. I grabbed my breasts to keep them from rocking, tweaking the nipples, the pain a titillating counterpoint to the thrill of his thrusts.

He began to move harder, entering deeper as I bucked under him. The door was open but I wasn't trying to be quiet—I couldn't have even if I'd wanted to. I was building again and there was nothing I wanted to do more than scream my pleasure to the world. I began to cry out— let it echo over the entire city if it must.

I could feel his member thick within me. I could feel its slide as it pounded in, then the slap of him against my legs as the motion stopped and it reversed. I wanted more.

I rolled over, gasping, onto my hands and knees. He seized my hips. And then he was rocking into me, my body jolting forward with the motion, breasts swinging freely as my hand found that pearl between my legs and began to stroke.

I could feel him sliding in and out, in and out. I couldn't take it. It felt so good...

Within moments of his entry I was convulsing upon his member once more; my fingers paused to press that special spot of mine deeply while his legs drove shudders from my hips to my shoulders.

I collapsed onto my forearms, but he wasn't ready to stop. After a brief pause, enough only for me to catch my breath, he started again—his hard, strong, ready member quickly renewing the thrill of contact; flesh upon flesh, body against body.

His breathing became heavy as I began to groan. "Roll over," he panted. "I want to see you."

I obliged, laying on my back with legs apart, thinking he would enter me like last time. And he did, briefly, before scooping down with powerful arms to pull me from the car.

My legs wrapped around his hips and he held me like that, speared upon his member, bouncing up and down. I cried into his shoulder, then again as we collapsed back against the cold metal of the car; our bodies upright but our thinking horizontal. My arms reached out to grasp the roof as he began thrusting. Even if he let me go, I would stay off the ground—held against the car by the sheer force of his pushes.

I was climbing again—the third time since we'd got here. It was hard to think straight, I was in my own little bubble of pleasure right now.

The cold feel of the metal on my back.

The weight of my body upon him.

His member driving deep inside, accenting every thrust with a delicious thwack as our bodies met. His arms felt so strong—like he could do whatever he wanted to me and I would be helpless but to obey.

And I was helpless. Helpless and hopeless and head over heels.

I looked up into his eyes. They were focused on mine.

And then he said three little words that were my entire world, and drove me over the edge.

"I love you."

I closed my eyes as the convulsions took me once more, and this time he came with me, my cry as I lost control sending him tumbling too. We fell into the cold, soft snow, and all I could feel was him inside me, releasing warmth into my very soul.

I loved this man. I wanted to be with him forever. I loved him and he loved me.

CHAPTER SEVEN

"So are we going to send her to jail?"

The 20 minute drive back to Booker's apartment had taken two hours, but it had been a lot of fun. It had taken another half an hour to make it from the car to the elevator—I was almost certain the bonnet of the Bentley was dented.

"Your wife?" I asked, bringing my attention back to the conversation. I shook my head. "It would be nice, but after 5-10 years she'd be out, angry and still have that pre-nup. We're better off holding it over her head—using it to force her to invalidate any retroactive action on the pre-nup. Maybe give her a couple of million to sweeten the deal."

"That's mighty kind of you."

I shrugged. "I don't hold grudges. I just get even."

Booker laughed. "I love you. And I can't wait for this divorce to finally be over."

"By the way—that reminds me!" I exclaimed. I dug through my handbag, pulling out a thick manila envelope. "This is for you."

"What is it?"

I shrugged, suddenly nervous. "The divorce papers. She signed them before she left."

"Are you serious?"

I nodded, biting my lower lip. A look had come over Booker. It started with confusion, then disbelief, and then transformed, when he pulled the papers from the envelope, into sheer, unadulterated joy.

He looked at me, and the joy clarified, then, into something else—a look that crossed his face and refused to leave. *Resolve.*

"Clara May," Booker began. "Since the day I met you, my life has been a rollercoaster."

He took my hand in his. "But one I wouldn't get off for all the money in the world. You've saved my wallet, yes. But along the way, you saved my heart."

He bent down on one knee.

My hand went to mouth.

"Clara May." He cleared his throat. "Will you marry me?"

EPILOGUE

"Hello? Is that customs and border protection?"

. . .

"Great. I'd like to report some illegal activity please? Thank you, yes I'll hold."

. . .

"Inspector Grayson, is it? Hi, my name's Clara. I guess you could call me a concerned citizen. I'd like to report a woman bringing illegal furs into the country."

. . .

"Clouded Leopard."

. . .

"Yes I know. They're on the protected species list. What's worse, she killed this one herself."

. . .

"I agree—sections 4.03 and 12.26 of the border protection act, at a minimum. She'll be arriving by private jet from France. Most likely wearing the piece."

. . .

I smiled as the officer on the other end of the phone thanked me. "Don't worry about it. I'm a librarian—following the rules is what we do."

AUTHOR'S NOTE

Thanks for reading *Billionaire by the Book!* I sincerely hope you enjoyed the ride. As an author, the four books grew into so much more than I ever imagined. I started just wanting to write about the emotional rollercoaster that was falling in love with a married man. But then it turned into… well… this—hopefully, so much more than that.

If you have enjoyed my work, you can find a link to more of my books on the following pages.

I'm working on a new book even as we speak. If you want to know about it the moment it's released (and get three free novellas), sign up for my newsletter at: www.nightvisionbooks.com/nikki-steele.

Nikki

FURTHER READING

You can find all of my books on my website at
www.nightvisionbooks.com

You can sign up for my newsletter at
www.nightvisionbooks.com/nikki-steele.

And you can chat to me in person at
nikki@nightvisionbooks.com.

Printed in Great Britain
by Amazon

16853695R00118